# Elinormal

# Kate McCarroll Moore

A City of Light imprint

Cross Your Fingers
A City of Light imprint

City of Light Publishing
266 Elmwood Ave. Suite 407
Buffalo, New York 14222

info@CityofLightPublishing.com
www.CityofLightPublishing.com

Book design by Ana Cristina Ochoa

ISBN 978-1-952536-22-9 (softcover)
ISBN 978-1-952536-23-6 (eBook)

Printed in the U.S.A.
10 9 8 7 6 5 4 3 2 1

Library of Congress Cataloging-in-Publication Data
Names: Moore, Kate McCarroll, author.
Title: Elinormal / Kate McCarroll Moore.
Description: Buffalo, New York : Cross Your Fingers, a City of Light imprint, [2021] | Audience: Ages 9-12. | Audience: Grades 4-8. | Summary: As she struggles to connect with her hardworking lawyer mother, eleven-year-old Elinor happily leaves ballet to pursue her love of writing poetry.
Identifiers: LCCN 2021026314 (print) | LCCN 2021026315 (ebook) | ISBN 9781952536229 (paperback) | ISBN 9781952536236 (adobe pdf) | ISBN 9781952536236 (ebook) | ISBN 9781952536236 (epub) | ISBN 9781952536236 (kindle edition) | ISBN 9781952536236 (mobi) | ISBN 9781952536236 (pdf) | ISBN 9781952536236 (nook edition)
Subjects: CYAC: Identity--Fiction. | Mothers and daughters--Fiction. | Authorship--Fiction. | Poetry--Fiction. | LCGFT: Novels.
Classification: LCC PZ7.1.M6555 El 2021 (print) | LCC PZ7.1.M6555 (ebook) | DDC [Fic]--dc23
LC record available at https://lccn.loc.gov/2021026314
LC ebook record available at https://lccn.loc.gov/2021026315

# Contents

## Part 2

"Dancing is just discovery, discovery, discovery."

~ Martha Graham

# Part One

# ONE

# Prelude

**M**y mother slapped the newspaper down on the kitchen counter.

"Well, will you look at that, Elinor? We won!"

I looked up from my cereal, to see what she was so excited about. She usually just paced the kitchen with her Bluetooth, talking to somebody in China or New Jersey – not to me.

She waved the paper in front of me. "Look – we made the front page!"

I squinted to see, but at first all I could see was a big blob of red in the middle of the page. The blob came into focus. The. Blob. Was. Me.

"For goodness sake, Elinor, stop slurping and listen to this."

I set down my spoon a little too hard.

"Budding Ballerina Takes Center Stage. Due to negative publicity surrounding its restrictive entrance requirements, the prestigious Ballet Academy of Santa Marita will likely admit local dance enthusiast, Elinor Malcolm, to its fall program."

My head felt all light, like it was a birthday balloon floating above me.

"Oh, and get this, Elinor. They end the article with my quote, 'We should celebrate uniqueness and not be held to some outdated, unrealistic standard of beauty.'"

Outdated. Unrealistic. Those words rang in my ears, making me even more dizzy.

"This is truly a momentous day! My baby girl is heading to the Ballet Academy. We'll show all those skinny little waifs what a normal girl can do. What do you think, Elinor?"

*What do I think? I think I hate that my mother is a lawyer. I hate that she made me audition for the Ballet Academy. I hate that they said I didn't fit the profile of a Ballet Academy student. I hate that she wrote that threatening letter. And I hate that now there's a full-page picture of me in a red leotard on the front page of the Times Tribune.*

"Um, what do I think? I think you're a very good lawyer. I better go get ready for school."

I stood up too quickly, nearly knocking over my chair. My head was still spinning.

"Please be more careful, Elinor. You're a prima ballerina now."

I walked slowly to the door, trying my best not to slump.

"I'll move my afternoon appointment so we can get you new pointe shoes after school today. Now hurry up!"

# Barre Belles

*he Ballet Academy is on* the third floor of a very old brick building in a part of the city my mother calls regentrified. Whatever that means. When you get here, you ring a doorbell and wait to hear it buzz. You have to push hard for the door to open, then you climb three flights of creaky old stairs.

A grumpy looking woman with long purple fingernails and a too tight uniform is sitting at the top of the stairs, reading a book.

"Excuse me. Where do I go?"

She doesn't look up.

"Sign in." She taps a clipboard on the table in front of her. "And go through that door." She snaps her fingers, then shoots her thumb over her shoulder behind her like a hitch-hiker, never once taking her eyes off her book.

It must be a very interesting story. Probably a murder mystery. For all she knows, I could be a mass-murderer.

I sign my name and think about saying thank you, but I don't. Usually people are surprised when you say thank you, and then they smile and say something back like *oh, you're welcome* or *no problem*. But something tells me to just mind my own business and go through the door. That's what my mother calls my sixth sense.

I thought I was right on time, but already there's a group of girls hanging onto a bar that juts out of the wall. The ballet room is huge. One wall is lined with mirrors, and the ceiling seems like it's a hundred feet high.

There is a skinny man in a suit and a bow tie sitting up stick straight at a big grand piano in the corner. He is running his fingers lightly over the keys, warming up. The girls are all warming up too, stretching in front of the mirror, making their bodies do things that are not humanly possible.

I scurry over to the opposite corner and plop my dance bag at my feet. I plop down too, and stare at the scene in front of me. This is worse than I thought. Way worse. In front of me are thirty very skinny girls in pink tights and black leotards. They all have hair slicked back into very tight buns that make their faces all look very pinched and very blank like they don't have one idea inside their heads besides, "pointe, pointe, pointe." They are real ballerinas. I am not.

Suddenly the room goes quiet. The piano player pauses with his hands on the keys. The girls all freeze in place. I make myself as small as possible here in the corner. I will say my throat hurts if they ask me. It kind of does anyway, so it's not really lying. I am definitely not dancing.

A short, fat old lady in a black leotard and a long swishy skirt comes through the door. She claps her hands three times and glides to the front of the room.

"Hello, my darlings! Let us finish our stretching and get ready to show that we're serious students of the ballet arts."

The music begins again and the girls are in motion, bending and stretching, going up on tiptoes, and standing like storks. The old lady raises her arms over her head. "Reach, reach, reach," she says.

The girls all reach high above their heads.

"Excellent, excellent!" the old lady says, clasping her hands together in front of her like she's praying.

"What lovely young women we have here. La crème de la crème!" She kisses her fingertips the way that fancy chefs do when they taste something delicious.

"Now, first position please."

# First Position

*ll the girls make a* vee with their feet, pushing their heels together and pointing their toes out to the side. Their arms are bent so that it looks like they're all holding imaginary loads of dirty laundry or heavy books. The ballet teacher looks as light and delicate as a butterfly when she does it. She doesn't look old and fat anymore as her back straightens and her skirt swishes gently from side to side.

I watch the girls follow along as she demonstrates each position. "Long neck, girls. Tuck those tummies in." When she calls out, "fifth position," the girls all twist their feet weirdly and move both arms above their heads. And when the teacher raises her arms over her head, calling out, "Reach, ladies, reach," she looks as light and delicate as a butterfly. Her arms seem to be dancing above her head.

I close my eyes and try to picture myself gliding across the floor. I try to imagine my arms above my head, reaching gracefully toward the ceiling. And for a moment, I can almost see it. I want to see it. But it's no use. I am sitting here, an invisible blob, on the floor of this massive mirrored room, pressing my knees into my chest, wondering how I got here and how I'm going to get out.

All the girls here fit the profile of a Ballet Academy student. I understand now what that means. They all move like robots, in perfect time with the music. The teacher positions herself in front of the tiniest girl in the front row. She stares right at her without saying a word. Then she points her foot, slides it a little to the side, and slides it back into position. The girl does the same thing. The teacher winks at her and a tiny tremor of a smile passes over the girl's face. I bet she's already the teacher's pet.

That's the reason I'm sitting on the floor. I know that if she showed me a million times how to do it just right, my pointe would still be wrong, and I'd twitch not glide, and I'd be just a half a second behind everybody else. That's not okay in ballet. In ballet you have to be perfect. I lower my head and hug my knees tight until the music stops, but I don't cry. Not even one tear.

A little later I'm startled by the sound of the teacher's voice shouting over the piano. "That's enough for today, loves! Excellent progress on those pirouettes!

You may be excused. Don't forget to say thank you to Mr. Phillip on your way out."

The teacher claps her hands again loudly and the girls who were all so perfectly robotic during class, turn away from the mirrors, spinning and chattering and giggling their way across the floor. As they pass the man at the piano, some of them stop to curtsy, and say in sing-song voices, "Thank you, Mr. Phillip," before linking arms and sashaying right past me.

And so, the worst afternoon of my life comes to a fitting end. I pick up my dance bag and get in line with the others as they head out the door. And no one says a word to me.

# Good News/ Bad News

After we got the news about the Ballet Academy, my mother had a meeting with the principal at school. I don't know what she said to him, but I got my schedule changed and I get to leave school after fourth period every day so I can make it to Santa Marita on time.

The good news – no more stupid flag football and dodgeball in gym class. The bad news - the Ballet Academy program will count for my physical education and I don't know how they will give me a grade. Based on today, I am picturing a big, fat F.

The good news – no more too-much-homework advanced math with boring Miss Simon. The bad news –

the only math class that would fit is general math with the rowdy class and the pretty Miss Chasten who cries a lot. Everything else will stay the same, except that now I will be spending lunchtime and the rest of the school day traveling to the city before being tortured in an itchy leotard and shoes that pinch.

It was only a week ago that my mother was telling my father in that bossy voice of hers, "Stop being such a worrywart. She doesn't need advanced math. In fact, I'm sure that the advanced choreography is equivalent to geometry. All those angles and that precision. Elinor's a natural mathematician. It will be fine."

My mother has an answer for everything. She drove me here today, but she usually has important meetings every afternoon, so I'll be taking the long way home. There's a Metro train that stops right outside the Ballet Academy building. I have to ride it to the rapid train station, then take the rapid train to the Park & Ride lot, and then take the MovingKids car service home from there. It takes a long time, but the good news is I can write in my journal the whole way home.

Sitting on the floor for hours was exhausting, so I hope I don't fall asleep on the way home and miss my stop. My mother says if you go past your stop, you could end up in a bad place, and that would be really bad news.

We did a dry run last week, and afterwards my mother told me, "You're a smart girl, Elinor. It's not a big deal. For pity sake. Just do everything in reverse. Instead of going south, you're going north. Look at the signs. Follow your nose."

I check inside the little zipper pouch in my dance bag for my Metro card, just as I hear the screech of the Metro train approaching. I climb on board and lean my head against the window for the first leg of my journey home. And guess what? I'm too excited to fall asleep, so I just look out the window and count the stops till I get off.

# Second Position

This morning, just as I'm heading out the door for school, my mother steps in front of me and puts her hand on my shoulder. I pop the last of my cereal bar in my mouth, and wait.

"That was JP on the phone," she tells me. "It looks like we're going to trial next month which means things are really ramping up at the office."

"Oh cool," I say. "You love going to trial."

She hands me my dance bag, and picks up her briefcase. "Right. But you know what that means. I'll be really busy."

"I know, but that's ok. You're always really busy."

Her hand on my shoulder tightens. I'm trying to read her look. It's somewhere between good news and bad news, but I can't tell exactly where.

"Look, the bottom line is you'll have to take public transportation to ballet for a while too. I'll make arrangements for MovingKids to pick you up at school and drop you at the Park & Ride. You can take it from there. No biggie, right?"

What my head says is, *it is a big deal. I don't even like ballet. I hate going there. This wasn't even my idea.*

But instead, I say, "Yup. No biggie. Can we go? I don't want to be late."

It only took one hour and ten minutes to get home yesterday, so that's how long I figured it would take to get to ballet. There was some sort of activity on the tracks though, so it took way longer, and I was frazzled when I got off the train and out of breath when I ran through the Ballet Academy door.

I was just signing in when three girls came pushing up behind me in one big clump. They were whispering and giggling and I don't think they were one bit worried about being late. I looked from girl to girl and they all just kind of looked like the same person, kind of like a three-headed pinch-faced dancer. And even though I looked right at them, they didn't see me. They just headed through the door together, a pack of floating ballerinas, and I knew I couldn't go sit on the floor and watch again today, so I just turned around and left.

Maybe you'd be afraid if you were eleven and you were all by yourself on a crowded street in a big city. Maybe I should have been, but I wasn't. I guess that's because in a lot of ways I'm not really your average kid. I've been packing my own lunch and doing my own laundry since I was eight. I have my own ATM card and I know how to make real dinner – not just frozen pizza rolls or mac and cheese. The truth is, the city is noisy and crowded, and real, not phony. It's way better than that boring ballet room with those phony robot dancers and that piano player playing the same thing over and over.

I'm not sure which direction to go, so I just do what my mother always tells me, I follow my nose. When I get to the corner, my heart starts to beat faster. Instead of more buildings, there's a little park. At first all I can see are grownups there, standing against the trees and sitting on the ground talking and singing.

There's a fountain in the middle, full of leaves, but no water. There's a group of boys crawling across the dirt in a path that has been worn through the grass – barking and meowing like cats and dogs, chasing in a frantic circle around the dried up fountain. They collapse together in a heap, whooping and laughing, big belly laughs of joy.

I try to imagine what the ballet girls are doing right now. I can almost hear the piano music and the teacher clapping and see the girls stretching in a long row in front of the wall of mirrors. I know they are there right now and that's where I'm supposed to be too, but I'm here. And here makes me feel so happy.

Behind the fountain I spot a girl sitting on a white blanket. She has long hair and a long flowy skirt that covers her legs. She is sitting with her hands folded in front of her like she is praying. Her back is very straight. It looks like her eyes are closed and she is swaying back and forth very slowly.

I can't stop looking at her. She is like a bush gently swaying in the wind. Leaves fall down around her, and she just sits. I want to get closer to her, but it seems like I shouldn't. I take out my journal and make a sketch. Underneath it I write, *Girl Praying.*

When I look up from my page, she is gone.

That's it, I decide. I will take MovingKids and two trains here every afternoon. But I will leave my ballet shoes under my bed. I will put my journal and my books in my ballet bag and I will come to this park. I will be happy here.

When I get home, the house is empty so I just push the code on the garage and head straight to my room. I don't even go downstairs and make myself something to eat. I never knew before how much happiness could fill you up.

I drop my dance bag at the foot of my bed and collapse on top of my covers, holding my journal with the sketch of the mystery girl. I don't wake up until I hear my mother's voice.

"Hey, ballerina, sorry I'm so late. How was your day?"

I open one eye. My room is pitch dark but I can see the numbers glowing on my nightstand clock: 10:31.

"Mmmm," I manage.

"Did you get to be in the front row today?"

"Mmmm."

"Did you brush your teeth?"

"Mmmm."

"You must be exhausted. You can show me what you've been learning in the morning. But now, go back to sleep."

Two things I know must be true. It can't be a lie if you don't really answer. And in the morning, she'll forget she asked me to show her what I learned.

# Human Tree

The next day I decide I don't even need to enter the ballet studio and sign in, I just get off the light rail train and head to the park. Walking straight towards me is the three-headed dancer, arms all linked together so that they take up the whole sidewalk. I have to stand in the doorway of the copy shop so they don't bump into me when they go by. I am invisible.

I make my way to the bench and plop down. I am directly across from the girl I sketched yesterday. Today she is a tree I think. She is standing on her white blanket, one leg rooted to the ground, the other leg bent in mid-air, her foot pressed against her knee. She is balanced like one of those birds that stands on one leg and her hands are over her head, pushed together like praying hands.

I look around the park to see what else is going on. There's a coffee wagon where people are lined up, two ladies pushing babies in strollers, a sweaty group of joggers, but my eyes keep going back to the girl on the blanket. Her eyes are closed and she is standing perfectly straight. Just like yesterday, she is swaying back and forth a little.

I take out my journal and sketch her. It takes all my concentration to make her look so still and strong on my paper. How can she keep her balance? Under my sketch I write, *Girl Praying, day 2.*

I close my journal, wait a minute, then open it again.

The praying girl doesn't move. She stands like a tree in the park. The leaves on the ground look like they've fallen from her. I wonder what she's thinking.

I add a swirl of wind to the picture I've drawn and put a bird's nest on top of the praying girl's head. I close my journal and watch her sway.

I decide to move closer so I can study her. I sit down on my dance bag right in front of her. Her breathing is exaggerated like the wind rustling through leaves. I'm sitting right in front of her, but she doesn't open her eyes.

I am looking right at the praying girl, sitting directly in front of her, but she doesn't even sense me there. She just keeps on stretching and breathing. Even my spirit must be invisible.

Finally, the praying girl opens her mouth and breathes one loud breath. She lowers her hands to right in front of her, then soundlessly lowers her foot to the ground. She bends both her knees, then lowers herself to the blanket. Everything is in slow motion. She opens her eyes and I'm looking right into them: big, deep brown eyes.

It sounds like she says, "in a gadda da vida."

"What?"

"What's the sound of one hand clapping?" She tilts her head slightly and gives me a lop-sided smile.

I just look at her. I don't know what to say.

She looks at me for a moment longer and laughs.

Her name is Indira. She is fourteen. She says she comes to the park every day to get real.

"What?" I ask her.

"Oh, you know," she says, "out there it's pretty hard to be real. Everybody expects you to do stuff like homework, and honor society, and ridiculous multiple choice tests. I have this teacher. Ms. Fris. No lie, that's her name. Everyday it's like, 'Showtime!' She has all these perfect clothes that all match, and she does her hair about a hundred different ways, and she wears more makeup than you could ever imagine on anyone, and every day I just look at her and I think *Ms. Fris, why the big show? 'Cause you know we're all going to end up dead one day. So why the big show?*"

I look at Indira's hands when she talks. She waves them all around. Her hands are in constant motion.

"And she cares so much about grammar. Always making sure this noun agrees with this verb. Like it matters! She always says this stuff makes your brain grow. She doesn't get it. Our brains are just going to stop functioning one of these days. Flatline! I'm teaching my spirit to grow. I really worry about some people, you know?"

I'm not sure I do know, but I think I like Indira. She is real. Even if she is a tree.

# Journey

Indira tilts her head and looks at me quizzically.

"So, what's your story, morning glory?"

I wonder if she always talks this weird and rhymey.

"You look like you need some serious chilling. Chillax," she says, "close your eyes."

I don't know why I do what she says, but I do.

"Ready for a little spiritual journey?" she asks.

I open my eyes.

"Uh-uh. Keep them closed. Roll them up to your third eye space."

This definitely sounds a little freaky, but Indira is so serious.

"Listen," she says, "in between your eyes is this cool space where your third eye is. You don't see out with this eye. You see in. Trust me on this. Relax and just listen to what I say. Start from right here. We're going to take a little walk across the park."

I make a movement to stand up. Indira laughs.

"No, no! Remember this is a spiritual journey not a physical one. Your body stays right here. We're just going to help your mind wander a little."

I put my hands in my lap and try to sit still. My eyes are closed and it feels like I am swaying back and forth just a little, just like Indira was doing when I first saw her.

"You're walking deeper and deeper into the forest," she tells me. "The tree branches are brushing up against you. You can smell the rich smell of pine, and every step crackles and crunches. You have to slow down and bend down to get through the tangle of trees. Stop a minute and get your bearings," she says. "Breathe in the leaf smell. Become one with the trees."

I sit up straighter. I feel like a tree.

"Ok," says Indira. "Start moving again. Straight ahead. There's a crack of light. Follow it. It's getting brighter and brighter. Up ahead is a clearing. See that little house on the other side?" I nod my head. "The path you're on leads right to the front door. Stay on the path. Look," she says, almost in a whisper, "the front door is open."

I am breathing really hard now, and my skin is tingling. It feels like all my nerves are alive. Indira's voice is so slow, so calm, and she has brought me right to the front step of this perfect little house. I don't want to open my eyes, I don't want it to disappear. It is so real!

"Come inside," Indira says. "Look around. Why don't you climb the stairs?"

She is silent for so long that I think I'm going to have to open my eyes to make sure she's still there. Instead, I keep climbing.

Finally, she starts up again. "It's time to enter the room at the top of the stairs," she says. "Look at all the things in here. Go ahead, pick them up, one by one. Touch anything you'd like."

I am surrounded by shelves and shelves. They are brushing up against me like tree branches.

"Choose one thing," says Indira. "Just one. That's yours to keep. Choose wisely. Hold on tight to it, and come on back. I'll be waiting for you."

Indira hums softly while I retrace my steps. Just when I sense myself getting back to the blanket, she says, "Okeydokey, artichokey. You're back among the living. Open your eyes, bright eyes."

I open them up and the world is changed. The park seems to have emptied out. There is a strange grey stillness settling down around me and my hands are clasped together tight in my lap.

"You better take a peek at the object in your hands. What are you holding?"

For a moment I really believe there will be something solid here in my hands, but it's only a memory that I'm holding on to.

"Concentrate. This is important," Indira says. "You're holding the mystery of your youness in your hands right now."

When I open my hands, I catch the glint of my smartwatch, and my heart stops. "Oh, my gosh! I'm dead!" I look up at Indira and for a moment I am frozen in place, my heart doing crazy flip-flops in my chest. Without another word, I jump up, grab my dance bag and make a mad dash for the Ballet Academy, even though I know my train has already come and gone while I've been sitting here.

Indira is shouting after me, but I can't make out what she's saying. All I can hear is the thrum thrum thrum of my pounding heart. I try to match the rhythm by saying, "stay calm, stay calm, stay calm," over and over, but it doesn't work. Instead, the little voice inside my head just keeps repeating a different mantra. *I'm dead, I'm dead, I'm dead.*

When I get to the doorway of the Ballet Academy, I am a sweaty mess. But then a miracle happens. Like magic, a light rail train pulls up, and I climb on. When I get off at the rapid train station to change trains, there's one stopped right there with the doors open, waiting for the transfer passengers to board. And when we finally pull up to the Park & Ride, I just click on the MovingKids app, and two minutes later a ride appears.

I need to pay closer attention to the world, I think. My mother always says, "When one door closes, another opens." Now I know that when one train leaves, another one is probably right behind it. There must be an endless stream of cars and trains getting people where they need to go every day.

When I get to my house and push the code on the garage door, the first thing I see is my mother's big old car parked in there. I'm sure she must be worried sick about me, but I know her worry will turn to anger when she finds out why I'm so late. I turn the knob slowly and enter the house on tiptoes, ready for whatever comes next. I can hear her before I see her.

She's in the kitchen shouting. "I need those briefs on my desk in the morning, so you'll just have to wait there until the courier comes. Call me as soon as they're delivered!"

It takes me a minute to realize that she means law briefs, not my dad's underwear, and somebody else is getting yelled at, not me.

I could go into the kitchen and face my punishment, but I don't. Instead, I head up the back stairs quickly and sprint to my room, where I drop my dance bag on the floor and belly-flop onto my bed. I lie there quietly for a minute to catch my breath, then I do something weird, but I can't help it. I sit up, clasp my hands together tightly, and close my eyes. I picture Indira sitting in front of me like she was earlier today at the park. I sit as still as I possibly can, then I bring my clasped hands close to my face, open my hands just a little, and concentrate. And there it is. The object that I found on the shelf on my spiritual walk is wedged there in my hands, as clear as day.

I stare and stare at it until it feels like the hairs on the back of my neck stand straight up, just like they do in cartoons when someone gets scared. But I don't feel scared exactly. It's more like that feeling you get when you're standing in line to get on a roller coaster and you sort of want to step out of line, but you don't.

The intercom in my room clicks on, and there's my mother's voice reverberating through my room. "Soup's on, Elinor! Wash your hands and come down to dinner."

And just like that, the object in my hands is gone. I get up from the bed, trudge downstairs, and enter the dining room where my mother is waiting.

# Warrior Stance

"Surprise!" my mother says when I sit down. "I decided we could treat ourselves to a special treat tonight," she says as she pulls my favorite sushi from the EatUp delivery bag. "Dad called and said his flight is delayed, and I've had a heck of a day, and I do mean a heck of a day, so…"

She passes me a California roll and my chopsticks.

My father has been gone for three weeks. He is working on some big project in Turkey, and he usually FaceTimes us during dinner which is his early morning which is pretty weird. Time is crazy like that. I forgot he was supposed to be here when I got home tonight.

"So, like I said, absolutely nothing went right today. The case is a calamity. JP is out with the flu. And now your father is gone another day. You don't know how lucky you are to be eleven without a worry in the world."

I stab a crab roll with a chopstick and pop it into my mouth.

"I could use a little good news. How was your day?"

I don't want to lie so I just tell the parts that I can. "We read a really cool story in Language Arts about a place where it's been raining for seven years straight, Mr. Chamberlain said I had the best grade on the Science quiz, and the MovingKids driver played Taylor Swift the whole way home."

After dinner she asks me to demonstrate what I've been learning in ballet so I stand up, make a vee with my feet, and position my arms like they did the first day in ballet. I know that's not enough, so I try to do some of Indira's moves. I balance like a tree with my arms over my head and then I do this thing Indira calls her warrior pose.

"Beautiful," she says, looking up from her phone. "You're getting strong. Now I've got to go work on lining up some more witnesses, so go start your homework."

The next day I can't wait to apologize to Indira for running away like that. And I want to tell her how my mother never even realized I was late. I guess she just came home from work and got right on the phone like she always does figuring I was upstairs in my room when I was actually running through Santa Marita all sweaty and scared. I want to tell Indira everything, but she is nowhere to be found.

Maybe she's just late today. I decide to sit and wait, and after a while I decide to try balancing like a tree. At first my balance is shaky on this lumpy ground, but then I figure it out. You have to make one leg be a tree trunk, strong and still. I push it as hard as I can into the ground and picture it growing roots that hold it in place. Then I bend my other leg and rest my foot against my calf at an angle.

"Breathe," I tell myself. "Just breathe."

My breathing becomes steady and slow, and I close my eyes. I am trying my best to be a tree, but instead, I am picturing myself in ballet. I swing my arms high above, reaching towards the sky, to the sound of the ballet teacher's voice in my head saying, "Reach and reach and reach!" I wonder what she'd say if she could see me now. I wonder what all those robot ballerinas would think.

I stand like that for a long time, until I get a tingly feeling, like someone is watching me. When I open my eyes, I see Indira walking towards me from behind the fountain. She has something cupped in her outstretched hands and she is laughing.

"Whoa! Got to work on your form there, buttercup. It's not supposed to look so painful."

I drop my arms to my side and plop to the ground.

"Oh, pish posh, Hieronymus Bosch! Don't look so sad and blue. It's called yoga practice precisely because it takes practice."

Indira drops down beside me and holds out her cupped hands. "I've got your whole world in my hands," she sings softly. She extends her hands till they are right under my nose, almost touching.

Sitting in the little bowl of her hands is something small and blue.

"Take it," she says. "For you."

I take it and close it tightly in my hand.

"Your very own bluebird of happiness," Indira whispers. "A gift from the universe."

A tingle of excitement runs along my spine and the hairs on the back of my neck stand up like they did yesterday. But yesterday it was something I imagined; today it's real. The little glass bluebird is exactly the same as the one I found on the shelf of my imagination. My heart jumps in my chest.

Indira looks right into my eyes. "Now, are you ready for the next lesson?"

# Unschooled

"I do my best thinking when I walk," Indira tells me, "so let's take a little stroll."

She adjusts her backpack and I pick up my dance bag. "I'm working on an important project right now," she says, "and you can help me."

"Oh, cool. I love projects. Right now I'm trying to figure out what my science project will be. I love science."

"Well, good luck with that. Science projects are lame. What I'm working on is not for school."

"Oh," I say. "Yeah."

"What I want to know is why we never get to do anything meaningful in school. I mean really. Ms. Fris had us looking up the vocabulary words from *The Great Gatsby* all period today. What does languidly mean?

Use it in a sentence. Then tomorrow it'll be on some ridiculous multiple-choice test. But none of the choices will be what it really means."

She stops walking and turns to look at me.

"You know, the supposed correct answer will be listlessly or sluggishly or something lame like that. And if I write in the margin, *Well, I think Fitzgerald kind of was a poet because he said they walked slenderly, languidly into dinner, and that doesn't really make me picture listless or sluggish, it's more like seductive, you know? I mean really, Ms. Fris, think about it.*"

She takes a deep breath and brushes the hair out of her eyes.

"They're walking in this slow, deliberate manner in front of the guys, kind of like they're saying I have you in my power, you know, not like I'm listless and sluggish, but she'll just mark it wrong."

She bends down and scoops up a little stone on the path, then slips it into her pocket.

"Plus," Indira continues, "I never even can finish the test because every ridiculous multiple-choice question needs to be explained, and I'll just end up flunking the test. Teachers want you to be so dumb."

The whole time Indira is talking, I'm clutching the bluebird in my hand, running my thumb over the smooth part where the head dips down, and thinking about the science quiz I just got an A on. Mr. Chamberlain said I had a great head for science.

"Let's sit under that tree," Indira says, pointing to a big oak tree whose leaves have already starting turning the color of fall.

She unzips her backpack, pulls out a bundle of white blanket, and spreads it on the ground. She kneels down, opens the backpack's front pocket and drops items one by one onto the blanket: a beer bottle cap, a Barbie doll head, a broken pencil, a crumpled dollar bill, a bird feather, and a baby sock. She reaches into her pocket and drops the little rock into the mix.

I sit down next to her on the blanket. "What's all this for? Is this part of your project?"

Indira waves her hand over the collection of things in front of her like one of those ladies on TV who are showing the audience all the things they can win. "Look closely," she says. "What do you see, chickadee? Can you spot the connection in my collection?"

"I see a lot of useless junk. Except for the money, I guess."

Indira rolls her eyes. "None of it is useless," she says. "These objects are the remnants of life. The detritus. Think about it. These all represent the biographical details of the park. See? Every object tells a story. Just think about it."

I put my bluebird of happiness on the blanket in front of me and pick up the little blue sock. "This is a baby's sock," I say. "What does it have to do with the park?"

She takes the sock from me and lays it back down on in the pile of objects. "Think for a minute. How do you think it ended up here?"

"Well, probably some mom was pushing her baby through the park in a stroller, and she was talking to her friend so she didn't see when he kicked it off and it landed on the path. Right?"

"A-ha!" Indira jumps up and points at the sock. "He kicked it off! He?"

"Well, um, it's a blue sock," I manage.

"My point exactly! A blue sock doesn't have to belong to a boy. That's so sexist! And you think he's being pushed in a stroller by his mother? What made you jump to that conclusion?"

I clear my throat, a little afraid to give the wrong answer. "I'm not sure. But every day I see mothers pushing babies in strollers when I get here."

"That, my friend, is an assumption. And a wildly speculative one. Maybe those women are babysitters. Or nannies. Maybe they're aunts or kidnappers. How do you know they're moms?"

I pick up my bluebird and stroke it with my thumb. I feel a sense of calm come over me. "You're right, Indira. I was assuming. My mother always says when you assume, you just make an…"

"Bingo! Assumptions are big problems in this world. You might think the baby just innocently dropped that sock." She picks it up again and waves it in front of me. "What if the baby flung it to the ground to leave a trail so someone could come to the rescue like in Hansel and Gretel? Or maybe it was used to conceal drugs or something in a sting operation. It could be anything. Don't you want to know who it belonged to and how it got here? Don't you want to know the story?"

Now I do. But before, all I could imagine was a mother and a baby boy and an innocently dropped baby blue sock. None of these other scenarios even crossed my mind.

"See, school, it wrecks you," Indira says. "It takes away all the interesting possibilities until there's only one lame answer. How sad is that?"

I pick up the bluebird of happiness from the blanket and grasp it tightly before sliding it into the pocket of my dance jacket.

# Gathering Walk

Indira is supposed to be writing a biography for English, but she has decided to write the park's story instead. Every day she picks up one object to add.

"See," she tells me, "the way I figure it is like this. If you're writing about a person, you take all these little scenes from their life and you string them together into a story. But that just gives you a bunch of snapshots of their life. It doesn't really tell you about the whole person. It really tells you more about the writer than the subject, don't you think?"

Before I can answer, she goes on. "I mean why do they write about the time it was so cold that the grandfather had to sleep on a hot brick wrapped in a towel to stay warm instead of about the time he sat in a chair in the library and read two chapters of *The Grapes of Wrath* one rainy Sunday afternoon? Both things are true. Both are important."

A squirrel scampers across the path in front of us and rushes up the oak tree. A shower of acorns land on our blanket. "I get it," I say. "I could write about getting the bluebird today or about almost getting conked on the head with an acorn. Both things are true and both are important."

"Well, I think the gift from the universe is slightly more important, but yeah, kind of like that. Anyway, it's the little details that make a story come alive. I tried explaining that to Ms. Fris but she just gave me her usual pained expression and sighed."

"She seems mean."

"Nope, not mean. Just sort of clueless. Anyway, I decided I'm going to write the park's story for my biography. That's my project. And it's not really for school. It's for me."

I hold out the little bluebird in my hand and finally ask Indira what I've been wondering the whole time she's been talking. "So," I say, "did you find this in the park, too? Is it part of your project?"

"Your bluebird of happiness? No, of course not, pepperpot! It was on a shelf in my room. I have a whole collection of little glass animals, and when I saw it yesterday, I just knew it was something you needed. I just knew it. Am I right?"

My arms are covered in goosebumps, and I can feel the hair on the back of my neck doing that stand-up thing again.

Indira smiles at me. "I knew you'd think it was special. Now, want to help me find today's artifact? We can start over there." She points to a bench where two old guys are feeding the birds. "The trick is to walk quietly and be patient. Don't pick up the first thing you see. You have to wait until you can feel it wanting to share its story."

We walk slowly, and I fight the urge to pick up everything. "Let me show you how it works," Indira tells me. "You have to listen with your heart."

Indira keeps her head down and her hands clasped behind her back as we walk and I do the same. "Tune out all distractions," she says. "Focus on the story of the park."

"I think I can hear something," I say as a big gust of wind rattles the leaves on the trees along our path.

Indira stops, and stands perfectly still, her toes turned toward each other and her hands on her hips. She slowly raises her hands above her, with her palms open and lets out a long, loud exhale of breath.

She is staring at something small and light that rolls right across our path, pushed by the wind. Indira tiptoes over to a tree where it's come to a stop. She bends down and picks it up gently, then holds it out towards me. It looks like a clump of string sitting there in her outstretched hand.

"Yipes, stripes," she whispers. She probes it with her finger. "Will you looky here? It's a little bird's nest."

"Wow! That must be for a very tiny bird!"

"Not even close," Indira replies. "This is an abandoned nest. Poor bird never even finished it. Blown away before it had a chance. This is the best discovery yet. You have very good karma, my friend. Exceptional karma, I'd say!"

Indira hands the nest to me. "You can carry it. This is a special day."

The path winds around a grove of trees and exits onto a sidewalk that runs along the outside of the park. "This is a shortcut back to our spot," Indira tells me. "This is the quickest way to get back."

As we are walking along, the weirdest thing happens. Three girls, all hooked together arm in arm, are coming towards us, taking up the whole sidewalk. Indira and I have to step off onto the dirt to let them pass.

They all have identical blond hair pulled into tight buns.

They don't even see me, but they look right at Indira. The girl in the middle says, "Hey, Tiffany!" then they all giggle and keep moving.

"Who's Tiffany?" I ask, but Indira doesn't answer.

She holds out her hand to me. "That's your signal to leave, I guess," she says. "I'll take the nest. You'd better run!"

# Family Dinner

When I enter my house, I hear voices coming from the kitchen. Laughter. And something smells really good. My dad is standing at the kitchen counter opening a bottle of wine. My mother is wearing my dad's *Kiss the Cook* apron that we gave him for his birthday.

"Well, there she is!" my dad says when he sees me standing in the doorway holding my dance bag. "Our little ballerina!"

"Elinor," my mother says as she opens the oven door, "go wash up for dinner and then you can join us in the dining room. Chop, chop!" She claps her hands together, just like the ballet teacher did that first day. "We've got some exciting news!"

"But first, give your old man a hug," my dad says. "I've missed my girl." He walks toward me and wraps me in a big bear hug.

"Oh, for goodness sake, Leo, she's all sweaty from dancing all afternoon. Not to mention that dirty train. Let the girl wash up." My mother pulls a pan of lasagna from the oven and sets it on the counter. Steam rises up, fogging her glasses, which she pulls off and wipes on the apron.

"Missed you too," I whisper into my dad's suit coat, then I pick up my dance bag and dash upstairs.

At dinner my dad pours me a glass of sparkling cider then raises his glass saying, "A toast!" He touches his glass to mine, then to my mother's. I don't know what we're celebrating but it's been a long time since we all sat together and shared a meal like this so it must be pretty important.

The candles on the table are real, not the fake battery powered ones that we usually use. Their glow is reflected in the mirror across from me, casting the room in soft amber light. I can see myself reflected there too and I like how I look for once. This is how happy looks, I think.

I pass my plate to my dad and he scoops me a huge square of lasagna. My mother adds a scoop of roasted brussels sprouts and a hunk of garlic bread. After everyone's plate is full, we hold hands and bow our heads. Then he begins.

"Tonight, after you do your homework, I'll tell you all about the mosques and the open-air markets in Turkey. I have a few little treasures from my travels for you too, but that will have to wait till the airline delivers my suitcase. Can you believe they lost it?"

"Not to mention they canceled your first flight and rerouted you through Romania of all places. You can probably kiss that suitcase goodbye."

"I have faith in the system. And, I believe in fate." My father takes a sip of his wine and pats my mother's hand. "After all, if I hadn't been rerouted, we wouldn't be celebrating!"

"What are we celebrating?" I say. "The suspense is killing me!"

"Please don't talk with your mouth full, Elinor. And use your napkin, dear." My mother says, refilling her wine glass.

"You're right," my father says. "I won't make you wait any longer. Here's the deal. You know how your mother always tells us that things happen for a reason?"

I nod, and look across the table at my mother who is smiling widely.

"So, I'm sitting in the airport in Romania, dead tired from being delayed. Just want to get home to my girls. The woman sitting next to me strikes up a conversation. Long story short, she's a reporter for the Boston Globe. Real reporter, international beat."

I swallow my mouthful of lasagna and drain the last of my sparkling cider. "Like Norah O'Donnell?"

"Sort of," my dad continues. "She's not on tv, but she's a very good reporter. I recognized her byline. Anyway, I told her your story, how all you needed was a chance and how now you're knocking it out of the ballpark dancing with the best ballet company in California…"

I put my fork down and feel my stomach flip over. The room begins to spin.

I don't remember much of what my dad said after that except it meant that this reporter from the Boston Globe was doing a story on kid activists around the country and my story sounded very promising. My story.

"You are quite the role model!" my dad says again, reaching up for a high five, "and it looks like you're going to be famous." I give his hand a quick pat and then ask to be excused.

"No dessert?"

"I have a lot of homework tonight, and I couldn't eat another bite," I say, pushing my chair in quickly and rushing up the stairs before they can see my tears.

# Tiny Dancer

he room is spinning when I flop on my bed and let the tears come. I think about what my mother always says when I cry. "Shake it off, Elinor. Strong women do not weep or whine."

I am not a strong woman, I am an eleven-year-old blob who hasn't been to ballet all week. But still, I wipe away my tears, and make a plan.

When I was five years old, we went to London for my dad's fortieth birthday, and my mother surprised us with tickets to the Royal Ballet. I can still picture all the dancers spinning across the stage. Giselle was the star of the ballet and she was the most beautiful person I had ever seen. She looked like she was floating on air.

"I'm going to be a ballerina when I grow up," I said when the curtain went down and all the people stood up and applauded.

I remember my dad picking me up and dancing across our hotel room later that night. "You will be the most beautiful Giselle the stage has ever seen!" he said as he whisked me off to bed. As he tucked me in, he told me how when he was a little boy his parents took him to see Giselle in New York and he watched some man named Baryshnikov dance. "I thought he was the most amazing athlete I'd ever seen," he said. "That man could leap so high, I thought his head would hit the rafters, and I decided I was going to be a ballet dancer too. But instead, I work for a bank."

He kissed my forehead, and stood up to turn out the light. "Sweet dreams, my tiny dancer. Dream big. Someday you'll light up the stage and your mother and I will be there to cheer you on."

"Dream big," he told me when I was five. Back then, ballet was my dream. So, I close my eyes and picture myself dancing across the stage like Giselle. I imagine my parents sitting in the audience and telling all the people in their row, *that's our girl up there. Our little Elinor is Giselle.*

Here's my plan. I grab my laptop and search YouTube for Giselle. I reach under my bed and get my ballet shoes. The leather is soft and beautiful. The music is soft and beautiful. Tonight, I will not do my math homework. I will not study for my history test. I will dance along to the Giselle videos and I will learn to point my toes and be graceful.

I stand in front of my bedroom mirror, reach up high over my head and sway to the music that fills my room. I point my foot and slowly rest it above my knee. At first I have to concentrate hard to get my balance, but then I can feel it. My body relaxes and I am calm and peaceful. I am standing tall and strong in the middle of my bedroom, eyes closed, arms reaching high above me. I can hear the ballet teacher's voice in my head, *reach, reach, reach, reach,* and I'm doing it.

I'm still balanced like this when the music ends.

Some kids forget to do their homework all the time, but I always do mine. I have never not done my homework before.

In first period, Ms. Chasten tells us all to take out our math homework. I walk up to her desk, and my knees feel all wobbly.

"I don't have it," I say, my voice catching in my throat.

"What?" she says while she's writing the answers on the whiteboard.

"My homework. I don't have it today."

"Oh, Elinor, that's not like you. Why don't you sit in the back and do it now? You can turn it in at the end of class."

Next period, I walk into my history class feeling better until Mr. Hoy says, "Remember folks, history is told by the victors. Will you be victorious today?" That's when I remember the history test I didn't study for.

I tell him I'm not ready, and he puts his hand on my shoulder. "Goodness gracious, Elinor, that's something I've never heard you say. Did you read the chapter?"

"Um, no, not really," I say. "I wanted to, but I was kind of sick last night."

"Well," he says, "you must have been really under the weather. How are you feeling now?"

"Still not so good," I say, and that's not a lie. I really do feel sick.

"Ok," he tells me. "Study this weekend and you can come in for a makeup test Monday at lunch. Why don't you sit in the back and try to do some reading now?"

I guess when you are a very good student, you can get away with anything.

# Changes

*A*fter school, I check my dance bag to make sure my ballet shoes and my leotard are there. On the way to the Ballet Academy, I keep going over my plan in my head. I will sign in and get in line with the ballerinas and I will follow the movements of the other dancers, pretending I know the steps. "Fake it till you make it," is what my mother always tells me is the key to success, so that's just what I'll do.

I'm a little bit early when I get there, and something doesn't feel quite right, but I can't quite put my finger on it. Maybe it's because I sort of lied to my teachers today and got away with it, but something just feels wrong.

I pick up the clipboard with the sign-in sheet and the security guard looks up at me and smiles. "Good afternoon, young lady," she says and winks at me. Strange.

My eyes run down the sign-in sheet and back up again to the top. I am looking for *Malcolm, Elinor*, but it's not there. That wobbly knee feeling I had in math this morning comes back.

"Um?" I croak.

"Something wrong?" She is still looking at me with a knowing smile.

"I don't see my name. I can't sign in."

She takes the clipboard from me. "And you are?"

"Elinor. Elinor Malcolm."

"Malcolm, Malcolm. Let's see. Nope. Not on the list."

I am trying hard not to cry. Strong women don't weep or whine.

"Don't worry, miss. Not a big deal. What we're gonna do here is have you wait over there till I get the rest of these girls signed in. Then I'll call the office and find out what's what."

I am frozen in place.

"Come on, out of the way, miss. Wait over there. You're holding up my line."

I back out of the line and lean against the back wall. When the line presses forward and blocks my view of the guard, I do the only sensible thing I can think of. I fly down the stairs and push through the door to the sidewalk. I run as fast as I can to find Indira, who is sitting like a statue in front of the fountain.

When I plop down beside her, she opens her eyes, and stands up.

I stay sitting on the ground, all sweaty and confused. That's when all my troubles come tumbling out at once. Indira stands perfectly still and listens, then she smiles at me and nods, turns around, and walks away down the path.

"Indira!" I shout. Where are you going? Wait up!"

She stops suddenly and whirls around. "Who are you?" she asks.

"Indira, don't do this to me. You know who I am. I'm Elinor."

I spring up and run to where she is standing in the middle of the path. She's not smiling anymore. She puts her hands on my shoulders and gives them a little squeeze. "Really, who are you?" she asks while staring deep into my eyes. "Elinor who? I can't help you with this one, kiddo. You're on your own, and you know what to do."

She turns once more and walks away. I have never felt so alone. I am standing in the middle of a winding path, in the middle of the park, in the middle of the city, and without warning, hot tears start falling.

"You have to help me, Indira. I don't know what to do." My eyes are so blurry that it looks like she is floating away. I feel rooted to the ground. "Please help me!"

Indira keeps walking and doesn't turn around. Her voice is carried back to me on the wind. "Help yourself," the wind hisses. "Help yourself."

I stand there for a long time trying to imagine what will happen next. Everything has changed. A big gust of wind rattles the leaves on the trees along the path, and a flurry of red and gold dances and swirls in front of me. I reach out and grab an enormous red leaf as it floats to the ground. It is the most beautiful bright red, shiny and bright. But when I turn it over, I see that the other side is already mottled brown. It is just one leaf, but it seems important. How can something look so colorful and alive on one side, and so dull and dead when you flip it over?

I don't know what else to do, so I sit back down and wipe away my tears. I reach into the zipper pocket of my dance bag and root around until I feel the little bluebird there. It is still a mystery to me how Indira knew exactly what I needed then. I hold it tight until I feel calm inside. Maybe she thinks I need to be alone in the park today too.

I take out my journal and slowly sketch both sides of the leaf. I use my colored pencils to color one side brown and the other side bright red. Next to the dead-looking side, I write, "This leaf is like me. Dull and boring. About to crumble." That's the old me, I decide.

Next to the red side I write, "I wonder how I'd look with red hair. I don't want to be invisible anymore."

# Book-A-Look

My mother tells me everything always seems better in the morning, and she's right. At least today. It's Saturday, the sun is shining, and I woke up to the smell of pancakes.

"Well, don't you look chipper today!" my dad says as I walk into the kitchen. He's standing at the counter, pouring syrup on a tall stack. "Your mother's going in for a tune-up this morning and if you play your cards right, I bet she'll take you."

My mother goes to the beauty salon once a month for what she calls her 3,000 mile tune-up. I usually go with my dad to run errands on Saturdays if he's not playing golf.

"Wait till she gets off the phone and you can ask her. Want one of my special chocolate chip pancakes?"

I can hear my mother in the other room, yelling at someone on the other end. "There are leaves all over the lawn and the gardener was just here yesterday. Yes, I know it's been windy, but I will not have my yard looking like a jungle. I expect this to be cleaned up when I get home this afternoon. And you can have him cut back the rose bushes too. They're way too scraggly."

I tiptoe into her office just as she's hanging up. "Mom?"

"Just a minute. One more quick call." She starts punching numbers again. "Finish your breakfast."

I head back to the kitchen where a steaming stack of chocolaty pancakes is waiting.

An hour later, we're in the car zipping along the freeway, heading to the fancy salon in the city.

"Aren't you excited about our special day? The two Malcolm ladies getting the works!" my mother says.

I'm excited, but I probably shouldn't have eaten so many pancakes. "Yeah, just feeling a little carsick. Can I roll my window down?"

"For goodness sake, Elinor. You can't open the window on the freeway. Just take some deep breaths."

I do and it does help a little bit. Then I reach into my pocket and rub my little bluebird of happiness with my thumb.

"I called ahead this morning and told Traci I wanted you to get the princess treatment. Hair, nails, maybe even a little lip gloss and mascara. They sell cute little tops there too."

She's in such a good mood. I can't believe my luck.

"I was thinking maybe I might dye my hair," I blurt out.

"Great minds think alike," she says. "Maybe lighten you up a bit."

I twirl the ends of my hair as we reach the exit ramp. It's hard to believe this is the same city where the Ballet Academy is. My mother says this is the ritzy part of town. This is where the money lives, she tells me. She stops the car in front of a fancy building and a teenage boy wearing a tan uniform takes our keys and passes my mother a card. "Welcome to Book-A-Look, ladies," he says. Have a wonderful experience."

Inside, we are greeted by a girl with spiky red hair who ushers us into a waiting room. "I'm Annie. What's your pleasure this morning?" she asks. "Coffee or tea?"

"We'll take two cups of jasmine tea, no sweetener," my mother answers. Then she turns to me. "Check out the bookcase, Elinor. They have such a great collection to choose from. And since you'll be coming with me now, you should take advantage."

There are hundreds of books lining one wall of the waiting room. A large overhead sign reads,

BOOK-A-LOOK PROMOTES LITERACY

FOR LIVING YOUR BEST LIFE

A BEAUTIFUL EXTERIOR IS NOTHING

WITHOUT A BEAUTIFUL INNER LIFE.

PLEASE HELP YOURSELF

TO WHATEVER CATCHES YOUR FANCY.

READ IT HERE, AND TAKE IT WITH YOU.

SMILE AND PASS IT ON TO MAKE THE WORLD A MORE

BEAUTIFUL PLACE.

And right there on the shelf, right in front of me, is that book Indira was telling me about. I pull it off the shelf and head back to where my mother is leafing through a magazine.

"Well, look at that, good old Fitzgerald!" she says. I excitedly clutch the copy of the book in my hands, *The Great Gatsby* by F. Scott Fitzgerald. "I guess this means you really are growing up!"

# Highlights

this is turning out to be the best day. I think this salon must be my mother's happy place, and it makes me feel like I can't do anything wrong.

Just as I sit back down, a girl with pink hair enters the room. "Hi," she says, extending an arm covered with beautiful flowery tattoos. "You must be Elinor. I'm Lonnie – I'll be washing you. Follow me."

I leave my book on the table and move across the way to a steamy shampoo room that smells like a summer garden. Afterwards, with my hair wrapped in a towel, Lonnie takes me to another room to wait for my hair stylist. A cup of jasmine tea is waiting there for me along with *The Great Gatsby*. I take a sip, open my book, and begin to read. I can't wait to see what Indira was talking about.

But it's really hard to concentrate on the first page with all the music and conversation happening around me. Plus, there's a lot of words I'm going to have to look up when I get home.

Lonnie is standing in the doorway when the girl with the spiky red hair walks by. They look at each other and burst out laughing, and Lonnie says, "I totally lucked out. Didn't have to shampoo that melon head today."

The spiky redhead gives her a high five. "I mean no offense, but what makes her wear her hair so short and severe like that?"

"Sshh, Annie," Lonnie laughs, "she'll hear you!"

Annie lowers her voice to a whisper, but I can still hear her. I'm definitely not concentrating on my book now.

"I mean really, you take somebody like Halle Berry. Well she's so dang pretty she can get away with that cut. Or Katy Perry with those big beautiful eyes of hers. But old melon head – she could use some hair to soften her up a bit."

"Yeah, well, I swear she still wouldn't smile," Lonnie says in a stage whisper.

"And for sure she'd still never tip!" Annie answers.

They high five again and then move away from the doorway, still laughing. That's when I see who they were talking about. My mother is sitting across the way in the shampoo room, getting her scalp massaged. When her head is wet it looks like she doesn't have any hair at all.

When I look back down at the book in my lap, the page is all blurry. People always tell me I look just like her. Does that mean I am just like her? I look in the mirror and try to practice my smile. I make a vow to myself right then that when I grow up, I'm going to be different. I'll change my name to something cool like Daisy, and I will never cut my hair again.

A few minutes later, we're sitting side by side waiting for our stylists when Annie with the red hair walks in with a stack of magazines. "I love your hair," I tell her.

"Thanks," she says as she arranges them on a table.

I still have the towel wrapped around my head, and I'm picturing a whole new me. "That's what color I'm thinking of making mine."

My mother lets out a little gasp. "Don't be ridiculous," she says, not even waiting for Annie to leave the room. "That is out of the question. A few highlights would look nice, but you are not going to look like a cartoon character!"

I can't wait till we're out of there and headed back home, but afterwards, when we get in the car (me with blond highlights that you can't even see), my mother says, "Well, that didn't take as long as I thought. So, surprise! We still have time to make it to the Ballet Academy in time to watch the professional troupe rehearse."

This cannot be happening, I think. "I have a lot of homework," I say. "We really should get home."

"Oh, nonsense, Elinor. I can jump on the freeway here, and it's only another two exits. We can be there in fifteen minutes and we're already ahead of schedule."

"But, I have a big test Monday, and…"

"No buts. No ands. This is a special day. Besides, won't the director flip when we tell him about the big story that the Boston Globe is going to run about you? Dad's reporter friend is calling us next week. We've got to line up those interviews with him and your ballet teacher and probably even some of the other dancers. I just can't wait to see the look on his face when we tell him!"

We pull into the parking lot across the street from the Ballet Academy. My mother hops out of the car. "Hurry up, slow poke." She is practically running. I climb out and catch up to her, as the walk sign flashes. When we get to the door, she pushes the bell, and waits. She pushes it again.

"Maybe they're deep in rehearsal and can't hear the buzzer," she says, glancing at her watch. "I know they rehearse till four on Saturdays."

"It looks dark," I say. "Maybe we should just go."

She pushes the bell again, then pulls out her phone and types something.

"Oh, for goodness sake," she says. "Just our luck."

It turns out that the studio is closed this weekend so that dancers can put on a charity dance performance in L.A. No one is here — not the director, not the ballet teacher, not even the security guard. I can't believe my luck.

She lets out a big sigh, and I feel like a giant boulder has just been lifted off my heart. Indira told me I have very good karma and I think it must be true.

"Well, now, just look at us. All dolled up with no place to go. What do you propose we do, Elinor? Your call."

I want to say I think we should kiss that locked door and go celebrate my great good fortune at a fancy restaurant somewhere. Catastrophe avoided. But instead I say, "Let's just enjoy this beautiful day. Want to go to the park, Mom? It's right up the street."

"Oh, for heaven's sake!" she says. "Why on earth would we go there? That's not a park. It's a homeless encampment. That's one place I don't want you ever to go near. Ever, do you understand?"

I don't say anything. I can't.

"Let's go get you some new pointe shoes so the afternoon's not a total waste. Yours must be nearly worn out by now."

I trudge behind her back to the car as she leaves a voicemail for the Ballet Studio telling them she has some great news to share.

# Out of the Box

Indira's in her usual spot in the park when I get there on Monday. She doesn't say anything about last week and I don't either. She just keeps balancing on the blanket; her arms stretched high above her head, back arched, head tilted backwards.

I put my dance bag down and take up the same position, facing her. Soon we are breathing together, breath for breath.

"This is mountain," she says. "Tadasana. Feel the strength inside you. Strength is beauty. Breathe."

We stand there like that, completely still for a long time. I already feel stronger. Indira shakes one foot, then the other, and sits down slowly. "Shake it out," she says. "You need to sit in your strength."

I sit down and tell her all about my weekend. About the fancy salon and the blond highlights that you can't see and the locked Ballet Academy door and my good karma. I tell her about the homeless encampment and the girl with the spiky red hair and the no tipping.

"Wait, let me stop you right there," she says. "First of all, these people here aren't homeless, they're free. I have a home, you have a home, and frankly, that's insulting. And no tipping, man, that's just plain rude."

I feel my strength starting to leak out of my bones, so I take a deep breath, and fight the tears.

"Oh, jeez, sorry," she says. "I mean that's your mother we're talking about. So sorry. She's probably a very nice person."

"She is. A nice person, I mean. She just has a lot on her mind most of the time. But that's not what I wanted to tell you. I was just setting the stage for the worst part."

Then I tell her about how when we got home there was a certified letter sitting on the kitchen table. How my dad signed for it because we weren't home, but he didn't open it because he would never open mail that wasn't addressed to him, even if it was about his own daughter. How maybe everything would be better if he had opened it instead of her.

"I'm not following," Indira says. "What's so bad about a letter?"

"It was from the Ballet Academy. It said they were sorry I had decided to discontinue my pursuit of ballet, but they were quite sure I'd find something else more suited to my creative pulse. Or something like that."

"No comprendo, senorita," Indira says, clasping her hands behind her in a stretch.

"They think I quit. No one answered the phone there, so my mother left a long message. It wasn't pretty."

"Holy cow. What did she say?"

"Something like, this message is for Mr. Tony Rabisham. This is Marsha Malcolm of Walters and Walters calling in regards to ballet student, Elinor Malcolm."

At that, Indira starts to laugh.

"It's not funny, Indira!"

"I'm sorry," she says. "I just never knew that was your name. Elinormal Calm. It's pretty funny."

"That is my name! Elinor Malcolm. What are you talking about?"

"Not Elinor Malcolm. Say it slow. Elinormal Calm. It should be Elinotnormal Notcalm."

She can be so weird sometimes. "Can I just please finish my story?"

"Yup. Sorry, Charlie. No more talkus interruptus,

I promise."

"Luckily, she has a big meeting today that she couldn't get out of, but she's coming here tomorrow. That's why I need your help. I think I should run away."

Indira moves to a kneeling position with her hands on her hips and shakes her head. "Wow," she says. "You really are in deep. But running away won't solve anything. What's called for in this situation is a little meditation medication. It'll fix what ails you."

"I don't feel like meditating. I need answers."

"Exactly," she says, "answers are just what the doctor ordered. You'll be sorry if you do something rash."

I open my mouth to say something, but nothing comes out.

"Get it? Rash? Doctor? I just love words. But seriously, Elinotnormal, you've got a major problem on your hands. And I do mean major." She reaches out and takes both my hands in hers and squeezes gently. "I get that this seems like the worst thing that ever happened," she continues, "but what would running away prove? I mean, no offense, but you're not exactly cut out to live on the street. And where would you go?"

I squeeze her hands back and it's so weird. I can feel her energy flowing into me.

"I hate to quote her 'cause she's so weird, but one thing Ms. Fris always says is you've got to think outside the box. You've got to use that other 90% of your brain that's asleep if you want to soar."

She has me put my dance bag under my head and lie back on the blanket. "Everything you need is right inside you. I'm just going to help you find it. Close your eyes. Now, toes go to sleep." Indira's voice is low and slow, mesmerizing. "Ankles go to sleep. Shins go to sleep." As I lie here on the blanket, every part of me goes to sleep, right up to my eyeballs.

"Picture the sky," she says. "It's dawn. A new day. The sky is just lighting up. Pink. Grey-blue. Golden. Here comes a cloud. Take one of your worries. A small one. Put it on a cloud. Whoosh – it's gone."

I can feel my heart pounding with excitement as Indira whispers, "Elinormal. Calm. Elinormal. Calm. Inhale slowly. Hold it. Hold it. Now exhale. Again."

I lie there in silence for a little while, then I hear her voice again, even more slow and quiet. "Here comes another cloud. It's small and wispy. Put a tiny little worry on it. Whoosh. You can kiss that worry goodbye."

I am feeling very calm and very sleepy.

"Ah," she says. "I can see a big dark raincloud gathering strength. Don't let it ruin your day. Take your biggest worry, the one that's weighing you down, and put it right up there on top of the cloud. Make sure to get the whole worry up there."

The world is perfectly still, so still that I can even hear the blood swishing around inside me. I can see myself lifting a giant worry over my head. Indira's voice is soothing, like a gentle gust of wind. "Got it all? Big whoosh. It's gone. Totally gone."

My whole body feels light, like I'm floating on a cloud. I can feel the sunshine pressing against my closed eyelids. My head feels hot. My arms are all tingly.

"Okay, mon amie. Time to shake it out. Jeepers creepers, girl. Open your peepers. Sit up nice and slow when you're ready."

Slowly, I sit back up. It felt like I was asleep for hours, but when I look around everything is still the same. There's still an old man sitting on the bench tossing bread crumbs on the ground to a few pigeons, there's still a girl sitting on the ground looking at her phone, there's still a guy in an army jacket pushing an empty swing.

"Well," Indira says. "Did you clear your head? Do you know what to do?"

"Okay," I answer. "I think so. Maybe I won't run away, but I think I should dye my hair!"

"Now you're talking," she says, jumping up. She reaches down to pull me to my feet. "Elinormal is out of the box. Let's go!"

There's not enough time to actually dye my hair and catch the train back home, so we do the next best thing. We pack up our stuff and head to the drugstore on the corner. One whole aisle is filled with cans of spray-on hair dye in every color – eggplant purple, grassy green, robin's egg blue. I pick up can of blue and consider it. It's the same color as my bluebird of happiness and that would probably be very good karma, but then I think about what Indira said, strength is beauty. Red is the strongest color. Red is beautiful.

I pick up a can called red-hot red. The girl on the front of the can has spiky red hair like Annie from the salon and she's dangling a red pepper into her open mouth. "Spice up your life," it says in big bold letters.

"This one," I tell Indira as I unzip my dance bag and fish out a twenty.

"Cool," she says. "You pay. I'll wait for you over there."

After I pay, and we're walking out the door, I swear the boy who just waited on me says, "See you, Tiffany."

Who's Tiffany? I wonder. But Indira just shoots me a look that says don't ask.

# Sing Song

If you have a dad who travels all the time and a mother who is super committed to her work, then you probably know what it's like to be on your own. Sometimes I pretend that I live all by myself in this big house, and it's actually kind of cool.

When no one else is here, I can cook whatever I feel like eating. Tonight I decide to make my famous fettuccine alfredo. My mother's text said she'll be home late, not to wait up, so I decide to double the recipe and leave the leftovers in the fridge. She'll be tired and hungry when she finally gets home and that should make her happy. I can't even imagine what she'll say when she goes to the Ballet Academy tomorrow to clear up what she said must be an unfortunate misunderstanding. Maybe she'll go easier on me if I make her something delicious tonight.

While I cook, I blast the music through the whole house. I like to turn the bass part up really high so the house feels like it's a dancing machine. It makes the cleanup go a lot better too, when the music is blasting.

I'm feeling a nervous kind of excitement afterwards when I finally head to the bathroom to use my red spray. I put an old towel on the counter and one on the floor. Taylor comes on just as I start to spray. Her voice echoes through the whole house and I'm singing along real loud, *"So oh-oh, oh-oh, oh-oh, oh-oh, oh-oh You need to calm down, you're being too loud."*

I sing and I spray and I see myself changing right before my eyes. My hair goes from mousy brown with highlights that you can't even see to fire engine red. I lean in close to the mirror and stare.

Last week Indira asked me who I was, and it made me so mad and confused. Now I'm looking hard at myself and I can see who I am. I am Elinor Malcolm and I am not who my parents think I am. I am not a ballerina. Sometimes I don't do my homework. My best friend is a girl named Indira. I have red hair.

I keep staring at myself in the mirror for a long time. I look older. I never noticed before that my eyes have little flecks of gold in them. Yesterday my hair was dull and my eyes were boring. Everything about me is changing.

I should be doing my homework, but instead I take out my journal. I sketch my hand, palm up. I spend a long time on it, noticing all the little lines that I never really paid attention to before. There are hundreds of little crisscrossing lines that are mine alone. I can't believe they've been here all along but I never paid attention. They tell the story of me.

I take out my little bluebird of happiness and study it closely, then I draw it in the center of my hand sketch. While I'm drawing, a poem pops into my head and I write it next to my sketch.

> *Seasons change and so do I*
> *This little bird just wants to fly*
> *It has to leave the nest one day*
> *To see the world and fly away*
> *Away she'll fly with open wings*
> *Its happy heart just sings and sings*

I read it out loud over and over. It has rhythm and rhyme, just like a Taylor Swift song. One thing I am really good at is poetry, but I don't think my parents know that about me either. Maybe I should get a guitar and put my poems to music.

I spend the rest of the night sketching and singing, then go downstairs to check all the lights and the locks once more before heading to bed. I set the alarm on my phone and climb under the covers where it's always safe and warm.

It's not that late, but tomorrow is going to be a big day. My mother always says, "Tomorrow is the first day of the rest of your life." That never made sense before, but tonight I get it. Tomorrow things will be different. Really different.

I think of another poem as I'm turning out the light, but I don't want to get out from this warm space, so I don't write it down. I just say it out loud over and over, like a mantra, until I fall asleep. Tomorrow I'll write it down.

> *Red hair, red hair on top of my head*
> *I'm not sleepy but it's time for bed*
> *There's no one here to tuck me in*
> *No one here to care*
> *But it doesn't really make me sad*
> *Because I've got red hair.*

When I wake up it will be the first day of the rest of my life.

# EIGHTEEN

# the Best Laid Plans

I wake up before my alarm and jump out of bed. In the bathroom, I'm startled for a minute by the girl in the mirror. I don't even look like the old me. Today is the first day of the rest of my life and I'm ready.

I make my way downstairs, only to find that the house is empty. There's a note on the kitchen table next to my cereal bowl. "Early appointment. Catch a ride with Mrs. Feinstein. I'll catch you later." I assume it's from my mother, but I try playing Indira's game.

What if the note is from a murderous kidnapper who's planning to attack me when I'm in the shower?

What if aliens landed during the night and they've parked their space ship behind the garage waiting to take me to their leader?

What if Mrs. Feinstein has been pretending to be my nice wonderful next-door neighbor all these years and she's finally going to unleash her evil plot when I ring her doorbell this morning?

I can really freak myself out sometimes. I have to do that mountain thing for a minute there in the middle of the kitchen, breathing and saying it slowly, Elinormal. Calm. Elinormal. Calm. I have learned so much from Indira. It really does work.

I open the refrigerator to get milk for my cereal. The leftover fettuccine is still there. I wonder if she ever even saw it there last night. I should have left her a note.

Mrs. Feinstein is in her driveway when I get to her house, and her car is running. She acts surprised to see me, but she doesn't mention my hair, just says, "It would be nice if your mother warned me that you'd need a ride this morning. It's a good thing you caught me. I was just leaving for Zumba." She doesn't say another word to me the whole way to school.

If Andrea Romero came to school with red hair, the whole building would be buzzing. She'd probably get sent to the principal's office for causing a commotion and then her mother would have to come get her, just like when she wears those tiny shirts to school and she has to go home to change. It happens every week. Some of the boys in my class even take bets on what she'll do to get sent home next.

But here's what happens when I come to school with bright red hair. Ms. Chasten says, "Getting ready for Halloween, Elinor? I can't wait to see your costume tomorrow. Let me guess, Little Mermaid?"

I have never ever forgotten about Halloween before. It's my favorite day of the whole year. I love getting dressed up to become someone completely different. Last year my whole family went trick-or-treating together at the Country Club. I was Wednesday, my mother was Morticia and my father was Lurch from the Addams family. It was so much fun. We haven't even talked about what we're going to be this year. It's tomorrow, and I totally forgot.

For brunch recess I go to the library to help the librarian, old Mrs. Dickens, shelve books. She usually lets me check out an extra book as a reward for working. When I come in today, she looks at me like something's different, but then she says, "My goodness, Elinor. You sure are getting tall." I brush my hair back from my eyes dramatically, but she just smiles and goes back to arranging spooky books on the display counter.

I thought having red hair would change my whole life, but nobody's swarming all over me like they swarm all over Andrea. It's just the same old, same old and I am just the same old boring me. The whole day is boring until I'm on the train heading to the city. That's when I hatch my plan.

I figure if I am dancing when my mother gets there, she'll blame the whole thing on the Ballet Academy. "She's right there in the front," she'll tell them. "This certified letter must have been sent by some incompetent office worker. You really need to pay more attention to who you hire." She'll tell them all about the reporter and she'll make them apologize for causing our family so much anxiety.

So, I'll wait outside the studio until a group of ballerinas gets buzzed in and I'll head upstairs with them. While they're signing in, I'll go behind the security guard and sneak in. I'll start stretching at the barre with everyone. That's when I realize it's not going to work the way I'm imagining it. I'll look like I don't know what I'm doing because, duh, I don't know what I'm doing. Like I said, I'm no ballerina.

Another mother might see her daughter struggling at the barre and feel sorry for her. She'd say to the teacher, "I see it's hopeless. You did your best. Believe me, it's not your fault. The girl is just not made for dancing. We're sorry to have troubled you." Then they'd go have milkshakes and laugh about it, and the mother would say, "Let's find you a different hobby. What is it you want to do?"

But I don't have another mother, I have my mother, and she's still fuming about that letter.

What if I just run to the park when the train stops. I'll get Indira to come back with me. She is so smart, and everybody likes her. My mother will have to listen to her. She can tell her about the life of the park and how happy I am there. She can convince her that the Ballet Academy is just not right for my personal development.

I grow completely calm, imagining the three of us, me, Indira, and my mother, walking to the park. We'll get some hot chocolate at the coffee wagon, and sit on a bench. My mother will say my hair looks spunky and it's so wonderful to see how I've matured. Bluebirds of happiness will fly all around us while music swells just like in a movie, as the credits roll.

But, this isn't a movie. The train slows to a stop as the voice over the speaker says "Theatre District! Downtown Theatre District stop!" and I'm jolted back to reality.

# Stony Silence

I yank my dance bag over my shoulder and grab the handrail on the door of the train. The brakes groan and the door whooshes open. I step down and look up at the same time.

My mother is standing right there.

Her arms are crossed in front of her, one foot is extended in front of the other, tapping, and her mouth is set in a tight line across her face, but opens in surprise when she sees me.

I don't have time to run to the park or to dart past her to the Ballet Academy. She stands frozen with her mouth hanging open. I do too.

The next thing I know, she has her hand on my arm and we are walk-running away from the Ballet Academy, past all the dancers making their way toward the entrance.

She pushes me into the street, not even at the crosswalk, but right in the middle of the street, practically right in front of a bus.

Everything looks blurry to me. I think I must be crying.

My mother doesn't say a word to me until we get to the car.

"Get in," she whispers. The voice that comes out of her does not sound like my mother. It sounds like it belongs to a different person, someone small and weak.

She clicks the key fob and the doors unlock with a little beep. She opens my door and slams the door hard once I'm in, then goes around to her side without even looking at me. She pushes the button to start the car, and stares straight ahead. I have never felt more invisible.

"This," she says through her teeth, "is intolerable. Intolerable. All this trouble I've gone through to secure this opportunity for you, and you just threw it all away. Just threw it away!"

Her voice is stronger now, but still sounds like whispering. I turn my head to look at her, and I see that her face is wet. Her hands on the steering wheel are shaking. Inside my stomach, it feels like a war is going on. Everything is crashing together inside me.

"What were you thinking, Elinor? What were you trying to prove?"

I don't know what to say, so I don't say anything. I realize I'm shaking too. I want to tell her that ballet was her idea, not mine, and they were right – I don't fit the profile of a Ballet Academy student. I'm not like those other girls. I'm not a ballerina. I want to tell her about Indira. I want to tell her about poetry and singing and the real me, and I open my mouth, but nothing comes out. Not one word.

"You've made a total fool of me," she hisses. "Can you imagine what that feels like? That ballet teacher hasn't seen you for weeks. Weeks!"

I keep staring at her. She must be able to feel my eyes on her, and finally, she turns to face me. It's too warm inside the car by now, my seat is heating up, and all the windows are completely foggy.

My mother reaches out and grabs a hunk of my hair. "And now this. This…," she repeats. "What on earth is this?"

I think the best thing to do is just make up a story about how it's just temporary because I'm planning to be Ariel for Halloween. I just can't make myself tell another lie though. "Sorry," I say. "I like red hair."

Right away I know that I said it in what my mother calls my "snippy" tone. I didn't mean for it to come out like that, and I wish it hadn't. It's too late to take it back.

My mother looks startled by my words. She looks at me like she doesn't even know me. I think maybe I don't even know me.

Last summer we were sitting in the yard, reading our books and drinking lemonade when we heard a really loud thump. We both jumped up at the same time and there was a little brown bird lying right on the patio between us. It had flown into the sliding glass door and now it was lying there with a broken wing. Its eyes looked so sad and afraid, boring right into my heart. I started to cry and I couldn't stop the rest of the afternoon.

My mother looks at me with that same expression and I feel my heart start to break. She looks at me silently, then turns away. She turns on the wipers to clear the fog from the windshield, puts the car in gear and backs out of our parking space. All the way home I wish she would yell at me or say something so that I could start talking, but she drives in stony silence, and I slump further and further down into my seat.

When we get home, I go straight up to my room, but she doesn't follow. I sit by the door with my head pressed against it and listen to her muffled voice for an hour. I hear my name but I can't make out what she's saying. I just know she's pouring out all her anger and disappointment to my dad far across the world in Hong Kong.

I wonder what time it is there. I wonder when he'll be home and when everything can go back to normal.

# Darkness/Dreams

For Halloween we do the worst possible thing you can do. We turn out all the lights and pretend we aren't home. Last year when we went trick-or-treating together, we really weren't home, so we left a big bowl of candy on the front step with a note that said, "Help yourself to a Halloween treat, and make sure to leave some for the others! Boo!" But this year we don't even do that.

I spend the whole evening lying on my bed in my pitch-dark room, feeling empty. The doorbell keeps ringing and I can hear kids yelling mean things like, "What a ripoff!" and "You'll be sorry!" In the morning when I leave for school there are smashed pumpkins in our driveway, and streams of toilet paper hanging from all the trees that line our walk.

For days I just come home from school, go to my room and wait. I wait for dinner. I wait for bedtime. I wait for someone to come home. I am waiting for things to change.

And then they do. The red washes out of my hair and I'm plain old me again on the outside. My mother gets over her big mad, and we don't talk about ballet anymore or about how much I embarrassed her and my dad. By the time he gets home next week, everything will be back to the way it was before, but I'm not the same inside.

I can't stop thinking about the park, and breathing deeply, and Indira. I keep trying to close my eyes and put my worries on a cloud so they can be whisked away, but it doesn't work without her. I wonder where she thinks I've gone. I picture her doing her tree pose on the blanket like the first day I saw her there. I don't know how to tell her what happened.

A year ago, I didn't even know that park existed. I didn't know Indira existed. I didn't know about good karma and spiritual journeys. I didn't know about robotic dancers who point their toes while a piano plays in the background. I didn't know about cans of hair dye that can change your whole personality.

Every day, I think to myself, everyone is going about their lives, doing the things they love, and I'm just sitting alone in my room doing nothing. I need a friend.

At least I have my journal, and it helps to write down my feelings. I keep writing poems about Indira, and birds, and trees, and the life of a park in a city an hour away. I even write poems about a three-headed ballerina and a floaty ballet teacher.

I write a lot about my bluebird of happiness which does not seem to be doing its job lately. I keep it under my pillow for good luck, but nothing seems to help. Today I wrote about the cat that I wish I had to keep me company. I asked my mother if we could maybe go to the shelter and adopt a kitten, but she just said, "I will not have a dirty animal in this house, Elinor. You know they harbor fleas and their fur gets all over the furniture. That is out of the question."

Even though she said no, I can still dream. Here's my latest poem about the cat of my dreams:

*I keep a bluebird under my pillow*
*to help me sleep at night*
*when I close my eyes*
*a sweet dream*
*comes to me*
*each night*
*I picture you, kitty*
*Little ball of fur*
*Curled up tight*

*Sleeping by my side*
*Purring so softly*
*With happiness inside*

After I close my journal, I say the poem out loud by heart. When I say it, I picture sharing it with Indira on her blanket in the park. I wonder what she would say. I guess I'll never know.

"It takes courage to grow up
and become who you really are."

~ E E Cummings

# Part two

# Dancing Tree

Today is a day that I'll never forget. I woke up with the weirdest feeling – all tingly and excited. I kissed my mother when I went into the kitchen for breakfast, and made her a latte. "Well, what a nice surprise!" she said as I handed her a frothy mug. I emailed my dad good morning before I left for school and told him I was thinking of learning to play the guitar. The day was full of sunshine and the birds were especially noisy on my way to school; I actually skipped my way into the classroom.

Mean Christine who sits next to me in first period looked up at me when I sat down and said, "Hi. Cute shoes." There was not a trace of sarcasm in her voice. I have read about miracles before, and I think I must be experiencing one. The whole day feels like a string of little miracles.

After school, I sit on my bed and listen to the music from Giselle – even though I don't like ballet, I still love the music sometimes. It makes me feel all warm and happy inside. I take a brand new journal off my shelf and open to the first page. "I have been waiting for the first day of the rest of my life to be different. I think today it is!" I write. Then I start writing a new poem called *Indira.* I can hear her voice inside my head asking, "What's up, buttercup?" And I can picture her so clearly, standing perfectly still, being a tree.

> *Indira*
> *Once there was a girl who was a tree*
> *She opened her eyes and looked through me*
> *She taught me how to breathe*
> *She taught me to stand tall*
> *She said to pay attention*
> *It's her spirit I recall*
> *Most all the time*

Usually I miss her so much that it's hard to breathe when I think about her. But today, when I picture her, I just feel happy and full, not empty and alone. Another miracle.

I close my journal, get off my bed, and move to the middle of the room. I close my eyes and slowly raise my arms up high over my head. I remember my third eye space and I try to focus.

"I'm going on a little spiritual journey," I say out loud, standing perfectly still. I breathe in as slowly as possible, pretending that the air is a big drink of refreshing cold water and I'm very, very thirsty. I swallow it down deep and hold the air in my lungs while I count to ten. Then I let it out slowly, in thin little wisps of air. Elinormal. Calm. Elinormal. Calm.

I keep my eyes closed and lower myself to the floor. The music from Giselle is playing on repeat. I'm very aware of my breathing. I can feel my heart beating in my chest and I am aware of my skin and the hairs on the back of my neck. I start to shiver, and those neck hairs stand straight up.

I keep sitting perfectly still while the music swells and the clock downstairs chimes the hour. Outside my window, a tree brushes against the window and gently taps out a steady rhythm against the glass.

Suddenly, the weird feeling that I woke up with this morning returns, making me all tingly inside again. It feels like someone is staring right at me, even though I'm all alone. I open my eyes just to make sure. The room is empty.

I close my eyes again, but the feeling of being watched is stronger than ever. It feels like someone is sitting right in front of me, staring into my soul.

The tree outside is brushing its branches against the house slowly, gently, back and forth, back and forth.

I know that the leaves all fell to the ground weeks ago and that the branches are naked, waiting for the magic of spring.

I stand up and move to the window, dancing along to the music that the tree is making. I open the shutters and watch the tree dancing. I move my arms gracefully in time with the tree and it feels like I am part of nature. I feel so happy, like I am coming back to life after a long, cold winter.

I don't know why, but I want to touch the tree. I undo the lock on the window and push it open. The tree is dancing, I am dancing, the sun is shining, the birds are singing, and everything feels so alive and beautiful. I reach out and touch the closest branch. It's then that I see her.

Standing on my front lawn, skirt swirling around her ankles, hair blowing wildly across her face, hands clasped in front of like she's praying, is the best miracle of all. Indira is here.

# the Gift

Indira is standing as still as a statue on my front lawn. Her skirt is swirling around her ankles in the breeze as she stares up at my bedroom window. On this day of miracles, it seems perfectly natural that she found her way to me.

I open the window wider and call out to her, madly waving my arms. "Hey, Indira. Indira! Up here!"

"Well look at that – she lives!" she shouts, "Come see, come sah, Elinah! I come bearing gifts!"

I have missed her so very much. I fly down the stairs and out the front door, nearly bursting with happiness. This is a dream come true.

Indira laughs and tells me what a lot of trouble I am. "Jeez, Louise," she tells me. "Do you know how hard you were to track down?"

She takes her backpack off and puts it on the ground, then loosens her hair from its ponytail and shakes her head. "There," she says, "that's better." She takes a big breath and laughs. "Okay, so I asked all those little tutu-wearers about you, but they weren't any help. Like at all. It took me forever to follow your scent. But, now, here we be. First find for Indira's Detective Agency."

The words are spilling out of her so fast, her hands waving and fluttering in front of her. Her whole body moves like she's on springs when she talks. She pulls an elastic off her wrist and secures her hair back into a ponytail as she explains, "You'll see. I really think I'm on to something here. I'm going to call it Sleuthadelic, what do you think? Is that the coolest name or what?"

"Wait, you mean like sleuth?"

"Exactly. I'm a super sleuth, don't you think? And get this. I'm designing an amazing website. It's like totally incredible. Ms. Fris thought my park biography was so cool. She had me share it with all her classes, and now I'm mentoring all these kids who hate to write. I set up a site for teaching, and voila, now it's even better."

The sun suddenly peeks out from behind a skyful of clouds and lights up Indira's face like she is in a painting or a movie. She grabs my hand and continues. "Just wait till I post about finding you on my website. I'll be in business, big time. Indira Makepeace, super sleuth. Super seeker of truth and lost souls. This is life changing stuff. Ah, but I digress!"

She finally takes a breath, so I guess it's my turn. "That's cool, Indira. But why? I mean why did you go to all this trouble? Why did you come looking for me?"

I wonder if she knows how much I've missed her. How every day I wanted to come back to the park and find her, just to be with her. I wonder if she knows how much I needed to see her again.

"Well, duh," she says. "You didn't come to me so I figured you were probably being held captive by these people. Your spirit called out for me to come help you. That's obvious. And here," she says, unzipping the backpack. "This little guy needed you for sure. He was hot on your trail!"

With one hand she reaches into the bottom of the backpack and scoops out a little orange ball of fur. It is a kitten, so tiny and perfect that it fits in the cradle of her hand. Water springs to my eyes.

"Oh, my gosh!" I exclaim. "I've been praying for a cat forever. Like literally forever!"

"Bingo!" she says, handing the kitten to me. "Bonding time. Get to know this little guy while I try to figure out how we're going to get you out of here. What to do, what to do?!"

I wish I had all the right words to say like Indira always does. I want to tell her how much I wanted to come back to the park and how much I thought about it every day, but how I just couldn't. I nuzzle the kitten up to my face and breathe in the sweet kitten smell, and I'm crying happy tears. I just can't find the words that are in my heart.

"So, tell me," she says. "Like why didn't you just hop on that train and come back? Like even once so I would know what happened?" She is looking right at me, intensely. "I mean what have these people done to you? Has your brain been totally washed? What's up, buttercup?"

The kitten is purring against my face. Its fur is so soft and it tickles my chin. I can hear its inside sounds, a quiet little purr and a happy heartbeat. I close my eyes and breathe in its kitten smell, sweet, like just peeled oranges.

"Hey, wake up, shake up, girl," I hear Indira saying from somewhere that sounds far away. I open my eyes as she says, "Time to show me your room and work on fixing your life. Let's go."

We spend the rest of the day getting the kitten set up. I tuck him under my sweatshirt so I can feel its soft fur against me as we work. We go out to the garage, dump out one of the plastic bins of Christmas ornaments, and fill it with shredded newspaper.

"Voila, environmentally-sound kitty litter box," Indira proclaims as she carries the plastic box back to my room. "Paper, of course, is biodegradable, so you can just rip up yesterday's newspaper every day and put it in here for the kitty."

Indira moves into my closet and begins to clear a place on the floor. "Jeez Louise – even a movie star wouldn't need all these shoes," she says as she tosses them behind her to make room for the litter box. "What size do you wear?" she asks, holding one of my new leather clogs up to her own foot. Before I can answer, she is slipping off her tennis shoe.

"Um, they look like they'd fit you. You can borrow them if you want."

She stops what she's doing, grabs the matching clog from the jumble of shoes there, and slips them on. Then she stands up and does a kind of jazz walk across the floor.

"Actually, you can have them if you want. They look a lot cooler on you."

"What a gal, what a pal," Indira says. "Elinor of the 'burbs, she'd give you the shoes off her feet!"

The kitten stirs under my sweatshirt.

"Listen," she says, "I'm not going to take your shoes, girly girl, but do you think I could borrow them for a little while?" She hikes up her skirt a bit and does a kind of jig like those Irish dancers do. "They kind of complete the look, don't you think?"

I would give her anything right now. Pressed against me is the softest ball of fur - living, breathing fur. I've never felt anything so perfect. And it's all mine.

Indira clears her throat, kicks off my shoes and claps her hands lightly. "Chop, chop. Time to get back to work, mon amie. We've got to get this little guy oriented to your room. Put him down for heaven's sake, and let's see what he does."

I reach under my shirt to remove the kitty, and he sinks his thorn-like nails into my stomach. He is clinging there when I try to pull him away, and that just makes him dig his claws in even more. "Ow! Bad kitty, bad kitty!" He lands on the floor with a thud.

"Well, that was not cool," Indira says. "You're going to have to learn how to be a better mommy. Luckily, they have nine lives. But that might have been the end of the first one."

Before I can even start to panic about the red scratches that are stinging like mad or how much that fall might have hurt him, the kitten does the cutest thing and Indira and I burst out laughing. He gives a quick little kitten sneeze and shakes his head, then he hops. He turns around to look at me, and continues kitty-hopping across the room. He hops right into the wall, then gives out the cutest little mew and topples over.

Indira and I are laughing like hyenas. The kitten shakes his head like he's dazed, gives another little kitty sneeze, and hops straight into my closet. He is so little that he hops right into Indira's tennis shoe and promptly snuggles in for a catnap. We are laughing so hard now and I can't tell if my stomach hurts from that or from the scratches the kitten left when he fell to the floor.

Did you ever see a kitten fall asleep? It is the weirdest, cutest thing. One minute they are hopping across the room like a frog, and the next second they are sound asleep in a shoe. And the funny thing is, they are just as fun to watch as when they are hopping. We sit on the floor inside my closet watching him for a long time while I try to come up with the perfect name.

# What's in a Name?

"Finding the right name is important," Indira tells me as she pulls on her ponytail elastic and puts her hair into a sloppy bun on top of her head. "It has to fit."

I keep staring at the sleeping kitten and picturing how he hopped right across the room when he hit the ground. The first name I come up with is Tigger, because, well you know, Tigger in *Winnie the Pooh*.

"A little obvious," Indira says, "and besides, how many pets named Tigger do you know?"

Well, none actually, I think to myself, but Indira must know lots because she just shakes her head at me. That is a name she won't even consider.

Then I say, "How about Kermit?"

She raises one eyebrow at me.

"Because Kermit's a…"

"Well, duh," she says. "Of course he is, but it's been done. This cat is an individual; he needs a unique name that will honor his individuality."

I sigh and stare at the sleeping cat.

"Think bigger, Elinor. Leap, for lizard's sake! The name you have in life is very important to your spirit. It tells the whole world who you are. Not to be taken lightly, if you know what I mean."

I'm afraid to say the wrong name, so I just sit there quietly watching my kitten. My kitten! I never, ever thought I'd get to say those words.

"It'll come to you if you concentrate hard enough," she says. "Just focus on his catness, and it'll come to you."

"Why don't you name him, Indira?" I ask. "You're probably way better at it than me."

"Oh, pish posh. You're the mommy. Look at your wittle baby!" she strokes him under the chin and he opens one eye, sneezes, and then just like that, he's off to dreamland again. "What name does he need to tell the world that he's present and accounted for?"

"I think I need to watch him a little more," I say. "I want him to have the right name. I bet if I put on my music it'll come to me." I tiptoe over to my bed and grab my phone, then pull up my "thinking music" playlist, and there, right on top is the music from Giselle.

Have you ever seen a ballet dancer on stage? They move like magic and they can do this cool little jump where they lift off the ground, click their feet together in the air, and then land soft, just like a cat. It's sort of like the way my kitten looks when he hops, like he's a ballet dancer. He silently springs off the ground, clicks, and lands. I think maybe I should give him a ballet kind of name, but I don't want Indira to laugh at me again.

Indira stands up and walks over to where I'm standing, and she takes my hands in hers. "Let's breathe to the music," she says. She guides me back to our watching place in front of the closet where the kitten is still nestled asleep in her shoe. We do some of our inner peace movements along to the music.

The kitten wanders out of the closet while I'm sitting in that pose where you look like a pretzel and snuggles right in my lap. I can hear him purring and feel the vibrations against my leg. We're already bonding.

That's when it hits me! It's just like karma. I think about the world's greatest ballet dancer ever and I picture him leaping across the stage when I was five, when I believed that I could move like that too. My dad's favorite ballet dancer, Mikhail Baryshnikov, can jump higher than anyone in the history of ballet. I saw him do it. And I've never heard of a cat named after him!

I'm feeling the unique catness of the soft little

creature purring so peacefully in my lap, and I'm picturing Baryshnikov leaping high above the swirling worry clouds in my mind. I know my kitten's name. I will name him Baryshnikov, but I'll call him Bari for short. It must be destiny.

I open my eyes. The kitten is purring, soft and warm in my lap.

Indira is directly across from me, sitting still and tall with a hand on each knee, breathing slow and deep with both eyes closed. Waiting. I don't want to disturb her just yet, but the kitten shifts in my lap and I feel a very sharp claw poke my leg.

"Ow!" At the sound of my voice, the kitten plunges both front paws with needle sharp claws into my thigh. "Yikes! Bad kitty!" The more I yelp, the deeper he plunges.

Indira opens her eyes, slowly emerging from her trance. Her glance goes from my face, where my eyes are welling with tears, to the kitten, now arched on my leg, hanging on for dear life.

"Sharp little talons he's got there, doesn't he?"

"He hurt me! Bad kitty!" The tips of his spiky claws are still dug into my leg, but Indira shows me how to gently loosen his grip.

"It's a good sign. He's bonded with you already. Claimed you as his own. Just don't wear shorts around him for a while or your legs will be a bloody mess, Queen

Elinor," she says with an English accent. With that, she scoops him from my lap and lowers him gently to the floor. "Your subject awaits his name. But first, the bestowing of gifts."

Indira unzips the backpack that she brought with her and pulls out two wrapped packages. She unwraps a box of kitten chow, punches her thumb through the top corner, and shakes a few fish shaped morsels into my palm. *"Cat-chow,"* she says, patting the kitten on his head, *"so you'll never know hunger."* She turns the kitten around so he is facing my outstretched hand. He looks around curiously, then scoops up a mouthful with a surprisingly scratchy tongue that tickles and makes goosebumps rise all the way up my arm.

"Now you," she says as she hands me a round lumpy package covered with blue paper and thick tape. "A little tricky to wrap," Indira says. A little tag attached with purple ribbon dangles from the side. "Read it," she says.

*"Cat-toy, so you'll always be playful!"* I read out loud. I shake the package and hear a little bell sound. I start to unwrap the package, but Indira rests her hand upon mine.

"Wait," she tells me, "there's more. Read the other side."

I flip the tag over and read, *"For a 'Bari' special kitty."* The hairs on my neck stand straight up. I am covered with goosebumps from head to toe.

Indira is grinning from ear to ear. "Aren't you going to open it?"

I drop the package into my lap. "How did you know I was going to name my new kitten Bari?" I whisper.

"Yipes, stripes, is that his name? Well, how perfectly purrfect!" she answers.

"I know it's perfect, Indira, but how did you know?"

"I guess Bari is just the name bestowed upon him by the universe and the all-knowing stars in the sky. It's the name he was born to proclaim. It's part of his essence, his *joie de vivre!* And you, Elinormal Madre Extraordinaire, are just tuned in enough to know what the wind already knows. You are blessed to be this cat's earthly mommy. What a lucky little feline he is!"

My eyes keep moving from Indira to the kitten to the shimmering tag in my lap.

"And holy smokes," she says, "look at the time! Let's give him his toy to see if he likes it, and then you can walk me out. I believe my mission is fini, mon amie."

She takes the still unwrapped package and removes the tape and paper, revealing a little stuffed bluebird that she tosses to the kitten. The cat toy makes a tinkling bell sound when it lands, startling the kitten who springs back into the closet.

"Give him time," she says. "There's a lot to get used to. He'll be your trusty sidekick until you're ready."

"Ready for what?" I ask.

"Life in the real world," she says, stuffing her feet back into her sneakers. "I came here to help you escape but I can see you're not ready yet. But don't worry, you will be. One of these days you're going to fly! And then, watch out world."

And with that, she stands up, drops my clogs into her backpack, slings it over her shoulder and heads for the stairs.

# Bless You

It's dark outside when I hear my mother downstairs clanging around. I kiss Bari's cute little nose, then settle him in the closet with his food and his litter box and his bluebird cat toy. I take my softest pillow off my bed and scrunch it up for him on the closet floor.

"This is your own little house," I tell him. "You just curl up here and go to sleep. I'll be back soon, mo na me."

My mother is sitting slumped at the kitchen table which is strewn with papers. Her head is resting on her hand, and she doesn't look up when I enter.

"What's for dinner?" is what comes out of my mouth. I know it's the wrong thing to say the moment I say it.

"Is that all you can say? What's for dinner? How about, *Gee, you sure look busy there, Mom. What can I do to help?* Or how about *How was your day? Can I get you a cup of tea?* Or what about, *I'll get out of your way, Mom. I think I'll just grab a bowl of cereal and take it to my room?*"

Uh-oh. It's going to be one of those nights. "Sorry, Mom. How was your day?" She shakes her head, but still doesn't look up. "Looks like you could use a break. I'm going to just have a bowl of Honey Nut Cheerios, want one? We've got strawberries and bananas to make it a meal. Or I could make you a salad?"

"No, thank you," she says. "I'm good. Achoo!"

"Bless you. Can I just sit here and work on my math while I eat? I promise I won't bother you."

"Oh, for…" She's going to say something, but then she sneezes again. "I'd better not be coming down with anything," she says. "I cannot afford to be sick with this trial hanging over my head."

I take a bowl from the cupboard and stand in front of the open the refrigerator. Our grocery delivery came today so the shelves are stocked with lots of fresh fruits and veggies.

"All right, sit at the counter, but I can't be bothered with your chatter. Tomorrow's a big day in court and I've got to be sharp. You're on your own tonight, kiddo."

The hardest thing I've ever had to do is to leave my kitten all alone all day. I kiss him on his little whiskery nose a hundred times each morning before I leave. I make sure he's got food and water and a clean litter box. I've made him some extra toys like a ball of aluminum foil and a bunch of yarn and strings hanging from a hanger so he doesn't get bored without me, but still he looks so sad when I leave; I can't stop thinking about him all alone in that closet all day long.

He's really got this thing about sleeping in shoes, but he's growing so fast that pretty soon he won't be able to fit in mine. I bet my dad won't even miss them if I take an old pair of his shoes from the back of his closet.

Bari has been my cat for three days, but it feels like forever. It is just the strangest thing, how love grows. How did I ever live without him? I keep trying to imagine what it was like before I got him, and I just can't. I wonder if he remembers anything before me. He must have had a mother, and I know that usually a whole litter is born at one time so he must have brothers and sisters. I wonder if he misses them?

He kind of reminds me of Indira, in a good way. Like I know a cat is not the same as a person, but he is my connection to her and the park. When I hold him on my lap and rub behind his ears, he makes soft little purring sounds that help me close my eyes and relax. I can picture standing in the park facing Indira while we focus on our breathing and stand perfectly still in mountain pose.

If I could take him to school with me, I would, but I can't figure out how he'd be better off zipped up inside my backpack all day. At least there's plenty of oxygen in my closet.

# TWENTY-FIVE

# Action Plan

The best thing about having a mother who's so wrapped up in her job is that she doesn't pay much attention to my schedule. She forgets that we get out early on Wednesdays, and she never remembers teacher work days.

Once, when I was in first grade, I had to sit on the bench all day because she dropped me off on a day when only the teachers were there, and I forgot that her cell phone number was written on a card inside my backpack. Back then I was too shy to go to the office and ask for help, so I just sat and waited all day on the bench. The only good thing about it was that I had my library book with me. I sat and read all of *Because of Winn-Dixie.*

When I brought it up to the counter in the library the day before, Mrs. Reedy, the librarian said, "Oh sweetie, that's an awfully big book. Why don't I save this for you till you're a little older? There are lots of great picture books that you'll like better over there."

That's when Mrs. Minamide, my first-grade teacher, stepped in and said, "Oh, no, this book is actually perfect for our little Elinor. She's a reader." I'll never forget that. So anyway, I'm sure glad I had that book in my backpack instead of a picture book because I had to sit there the whole day and I got to read the whole book without feeling one bit sorry for myself. It ended up being a great day. If I had a dog instead of a cat, I'd want one just like Winn-Dixie.

These days, I have all my important numbers saved in my phone: Mother's office, Dad's cell, Mrs. Feinberg, MovingKids, and DoorDash. I keep track of my own schedule, and that's how I know she won't remember that I don't have school tomorrow.

Our teachers are all spending the day learning. Ms. Chasten said she'll be sitting in a desk just like us, learning new math strategies from a math guru named Dr. Numbero. That's not his real name, but he calls himself that because Ms. Chasten says numbers are his life. It would be good if he could teach her more about controlling the class instead of more about math. All the teachers will be busy learning at school, and I'll be going on an adventure. I'm going to track down Indira in the city.

Instead of doing my homework after dinner I do a different kind of work – I'm getting ready for tomorrow. I lay out all my clothes on my bed, then rifle through my desk for my park journal with the drawings of Indira and the leaf and all my park poems. I find my favorite gel pen, some colored pencils for sketching, and a little change purse for money, my ATM card, and my library card, just in case. I make a list of everything I'm going to need and put a check mark next to things as I gather them: flashlight, check; water bottle, check; two power bars, check; cell phone, check. Bari hops up on my bed and curls up on top of the sweater I'm wearing tomorrow.

I can't resist. I climb in next to him and rub his little back. Sparks of electricity shoot up and crackle each time my hand touches his fur. It looks like sparks of light are shooting from my fingertips as I stroke his head and back. Bari snuggles in closer, opens his eyes and looks right at me. His eyes are shiny green with little specks of gold. I try to outstare him, but it's no use. He doesn't blink, just keeps looking deep inside me and purring quietly.

"That's it," I tell him. "You're coming with me tomorrow."

I lie on my back and pull him onto my chest, and just like that he yawns, closes his eyes and crawls up till he's nuzzled right under my chin. His soft purring sounds like a lullaby. It's so comfortable and warm snuggled there together, that I drift off to sleep. When I open my eyes again, it feels like only a minute has passed, but the red numbers glowing on my alarm clock say that it's 9:07.

I feel groggy and want to just roll over and go back to sleep, but I make myself get up. I head to the garage to find something to carry Bari in if he's going to be my side-kick. I know my backpack or my dance bag won't work. If we'll be gone all day, he's going to need oxygen.

In the back part of the garage there's a bunch of labeled plastic bins. I find the one marked "totes" and pull it down. When I open the lid, I'm looking at the most perfect cat carrier. It's a soft sided cooler with lots of side pouches and a top that opens with a zipper. The inside is lined with shiny silver material designed to keep hot things hot and cold things cold. The silver material has lots of little holes in it that will make it easy for Bari to breathe.

I put the bin back on the shelf and carry the kitty tote that used to be a picnic cooler into the house. The hallway is dark and I tiptoe carefully past the laundry room and the kitchen. Just as I round the corner, the hall light clicks on.

"My goodness, Elinor. I thought I heard noises coming from the garage. What on earth are you up to?" My mother is standing in front of me in a red velour sweatsuit stretched too tight across her middle. Her hair is wet and flattened against her head. She takes up the whole doorway, and I am frozen stiff.

"What?" I stammer. "Oh, I didn't know you were still up, Mom. This is for school tomorrow. Sixth grade is having a picnic lunch in the courtyard. I said I'd bring a cooler."

"Achoo." My mother's eyes are all watery and her mascara is smudged under both eyes. "Well, I hope it doesn't rain. There's a brand new bag of chips in the pantry that you can take. Top shelf."

"Thanks," I say without even a trace of guilt. "Are you all right?"

"It's the strangest thing," she says, leaning against the doorway. "I've been sneezing ever since I got home again today. I keep thinking I'm getting a terrible cold, but when I get to work, I'm fine." She pulls a tissue from her sleeve and blows her nose. "I thought a hot shower would help, but look at me." Her nose and her cheeks are bright red, the color of her sweatsuit. "I'm going to see Dr. King-Fisher in the morning. It just came on me out of the blue and I can't seem to shake it."

"Well, I hope you feel better tomorrow. I better get to bed. G'night," I say as I push past her. As I start up the stairs, I brush a big clump of cat fur off my shirt.

"Elinor?"

I turn around quickly, clutching the cooler tight to my chest.

"I'm not going to the office before my appointment tomorrow. I'll drive you to school."

I swallow hard. "Oh, great, Mom. See you bright and early."

On the way up the stairs, I'm already plotting my escape. I am turning into a sneak and a liar. I wonder what Indira will say.

# the Cat's Out of the Bag

he alarm on the phone under my pillow rings at four a.m. and I spring into action. I grab Bari and put him into the closet where he can't escape, then I creep silently down the hall. I stand motionless outside my parents' bedroom, pressing my ear to the door and trying not to breathe. I turn the doorknob in slow motion and count to ten. Then slowly, soundlessly, I push the door open and stand in the entry in mountain pose, still as a statue while my eyes adjust to the darkness.

My mother is lying on her side, her mouth wide open. She is making soft little noises that sound kind of like Bari's purring, and she's wearing her purple sleep mask. I bet she has her ear plugs in too; I creep closer to see but it's too dark to know for sure. She looks so peaceful sleeping there, turned towards the wall on my dad's side of the bed, holding his pillow tight, like a teddy bear. I try to remember where he is this week, Boston or Bosnia, or some other place that starts with a B, I think. It's hard to remember.

I tiptoe towards the bed and reach for the alarm clock glowing on the nightstand next to a tall pile of papers and folders. In one swift motion I turn the switch to its off position and replace the clock, careful not to disturb anything. I take one more long look at my sleeping mother, then back slowly out of the room and pull the door closed tight.

Three hours later my alarm goes off again. I jump up, make my bed quickly, and stuff the bag of chips from the pantry underneath my bed. I give Bari a kiss on the nose, then lower him into the main compartment of the cooler along with his bluebird toy, a Ziploc bag of kitten food, my water bottles and power bars, then hurriedly zip it closed. I've already put my wallet and bluebird of happiness in one of the outside pockets, and my journal, pen, and pencils in the larger side pouch. I make sure my cell phone is on silent, and I zip it into my jacket pocket, then head downstairs.

My plan is in full swing. I feel like Harriet the Spy from that book I read at camp when I was little. I set the cooler down in the front hallway and hope that Bari can stay nice and quiet in there. I pour myself a bowl of cereal and read the back of the cereal box while I'm eating.

And then I hear the sound I've been waiting for. My mother's feet hit the floor and she's swearing. A lot of bad words come flying down the stairs. I jump up and click on the intercom to her bedroom. "Mom," I say, "Are you okay? What's the matter?"

"I can't believe it! That worthless alarm never went off and I know I set it! This #*@#! stuffed nose made me oversleep. I can't be late to the doctor!"

"Oh, my gosh," I say in my best calming voice. "It's okay, Mom. Don't worry about me. Just get yourself ready. I'll grab the bus!"

And before she has a chance to protest, I dump my cereal bowl in the sink, grab the cooler by the front door, and take off running. When I get to the corner, I pull out my phone, pull up the MovingKids app, and hail a ride to the train station.

My heart is pounding with excitement, but I don't want to take calming breaths this morning. I want to feel all the feels. I take a look all around, making sure to be aware of my surroundings, like my mother always tells me. The early morning people look different than the people who used to ride the train after school. Everybody here is dressed up and distracted, reading the news on their phones or talking loudly on their Bluetooth devices as they climb aboard the train.

As soon as I am on board, I'm squooshed. There are so many people standing and holding on to the straps that dangle from the ceiling while they continue to read and talk to invisible people. I can't reach the straps, and the seats are all full so I kind of lean against the lady next to me for balance. Every time the train screeches to a stop, more people pile on and a few people get off. There's a guy with a bicycle bumping into everyone, and my sweater feels super itchy against my neck.

I manage to get off with a huge clump of people to transfer to the light rail train that's waiting in the city center station, and we all pile on that together. After only two stops, the conductor calls out "Theatre District!" I push my way to the door, clutching my cooler tight, but I can't get out before the door closes and the train lurches forward again. I am stuck, smooshed up against somebody's itchy black coat until the next stop, where I get pushed off the train with the crowd in an unfamiliar part of the city.

I don't know where I am. This was not part of the plan.

I make my way to the escalator, up and out to the bright morning. From the cooler, I hear a faint mewing. Bari must sense the change in the air, because as I walk to a nearby bench to get my bearings, he starts scratching away and his cat noises get louder. I sit down and unzip the cooler a little bit, to let him know that I'm here and everything is all right. I should realize what a scared cat would do in a situation like this, but it doesn't occur to me until it's too late.

The second I start unzipping the top of the cooler, Bari springs out like a tiger jumping through a flaming hoop, and he takes off. Without even thinking, I take off too, chasing him through a crowd of people down a busy city street.

# TWENTY-SEVEN

# Not So Random Acts

Just as I'm about to dart across the street following Bari, I am startled by a city bus squealing to a stop in front of me. Like lights being clicked on one by one in a darkened house, the city comes sharply into focus. There's this bus, then all these cars honking, rushing office workers moving along side by side, a trumpet player greeting people on the corner, a wall of windows on a tall building with a doorman on one side of me, and right next to me on the other side, a green kiosk piled high with magazines and newspapers. I freeze in my tracks. What chance does a little orange kitty have in all this chaos?

A sick feeling rises from the bottom of my stomach and slowly fills up my insides with fear and sorrow. I just stand there on the curb, holding the cooler, unable to move.

The man selling newspapers in the kiosk calls out to me. "Hey, young lady, you lose something?"

I look up to see him walking towards me, with a spring in his step and a broad smile across his face. He's got a newspaper under one arm, and a ball of orange fur held tightly against his chest.

"Bari!"

"This your beast?" he says, nuzzling Bari under his chin.

"Thank you, thank you!" I pant. "I can't believe it. I thought he was gone for good."

"City's no place for a little kitten to be roamin' around, for crying out loud. Traffic don't even stop for pedestrians, never mind a little helpless creature like this guy."

He tells me to come with him so he can get me a leash. I follow him to the newsstand where he cuts a long piece of twine from around a stack of newspapers and loops it around the kitten's collar, then ties a double knot.

"This should do it," he says. "You shouldn't let him out again, but at least if you do, you'll know he's safe." He kisses Bari right on the nose and hands him back to me. "And you be safe too, young lady. People don't look out for each other these days, so you got to look out for yourself."

"I will," I tell him. "How much do I owe you?"

"Are you kiddin'? Consider this my random act of kindness for the day. You take care to pass it on." He winks at me and his mustache twitches when he smiles, revealing a big gold tooth right in front.

"Can I buy a paper then?" I ask, but already he has turned to talk to someone else.

I lower Bari carefully back into the cooler, and make sure to zip it all the way closed. Then I stuff five dollars into the coffee can on the kiosk's ledge and help myself to a copy of *The Santa Marita Spirit.* I fold it into a pocket on the side of the cooler and start walking down the sunshine side of the street.

# TWENTY-EIGHT

# Sidewalk Story

I am sure I'm walking in the direction of the park because I'm following my nose, but after twenty minutes carrying a cooler full of kitten, I'm not so sure. The longer I walk, the heavier it seems to get, and nothing looks familiar. I decide it's time to take a break, find a patch of sunlight, and plop myself down under a tree. Lots of people are doing the same thing, leaning against buildings and trees and bike racks, and no one seems to care. Some people even look like they're asleep. There are almost as many people on the ground as there are people walking by.

I lean into the tree and look around. I'm already hungry and thirsty but I realize I made a big mistake by zipping my water and power bars inside the cooler with Bari. I'm not ready to go through that scary ordeal again, and I don't have all that much faith in a leash made of string, so I try to think of something besides my growling stomach and parched throat.

I start to daydream there in the sunshine and I remember that quote on the wall at the beauty salon, A BEAUTIFUL EXTERIOR IS NOTHING WITHOUT A BEAUTIFUL INNER LIFE. That makes me think about all the things Indira taught me, and I try to imagine what Indira would say if she knew I was sitting on the ground in an unfamiliar place with my kitten in a cooler and a newspaper waiting to be read. I bet she'd say, "Take some time to nourish your spirit with lifenews. Read all about it!" Even though she's not here, I can hear her voice, so I take her advice, and open the paper.

It looks so different than the one we get at home. For one thing, it is much thinner. And there is not one picture on the front page. Not one. Across the top where the headline should be it just says FREE.

Nothing grabs my interest on the front page, so I open it up. The first thing that catches my eye is a grainy black and white picture of a woman smiling right at me. She looks so familiar. Eerily familiar. Underneath her picture it says, BEHIND THE WHEEL… CARPOOL CONVERSATIONS BROUGHT TO YOU BY SHOSHANA FINKLE-WOO.

I've never been in a carpool.

I relax against the tree and start to read.

*What's a mother to do when her teenage girl's got a yin-yang full of angst? Simple. Just give her space. Let her breathe. That's what I do, and take it from me, it works.*

*In the carpool these days, I'm as silent as a lamb. Just put it in gear and drive.*

*Remember a few short years ago they were a giggling bunch of middle school wannabe's, spilling their guts on the way to school? Now I'm lucky to get a grumbled hello. But you know me. I don't mind.*

*Seems like they're just trying to catch an extra ten minutes of shut eye before I drop them off at school. The carpool is a sleep chamber these days. But like I said, I don't mind.*

*As long as I can go along for the ride while they become independent women of the world, I'm okay. I feel blessed to witness the transformation.*

*Luckily, I have other ways of keeping up with the high school scene, so I can keep you up to date. It's a mother's job to know what's happening in their lives.*

*Right now, it's Daisy Mae Drag time, a tradition that's a holdover from when we were all in school. All the high school girls are getting ready to use their feminine wiles to woo the boy of their dreams and ask him to dance. And for the record, it works. That's how I snared Chester Woo those many moons ago.*

*If you find out who Tiffany plans to ask, you can just email that good news to me here at the Santa Marita Spirit. After all, he could turn out to be my son-in-law one day. You never know!*

*Speaking of my Tiffany, allow me to brag just a bit. I've heard through the grapevine that she is quite the wonderkid on the computer. Latest buzz has it that she's teaching writing to a bunch of lucky underclassmen. Wonder where she got that writing gene?*

*In other news, the drama club is performing What's Eating Gilbert Grape next weekend, and the amazing jazz band is traveling to Tucson Tuesday for the Camel Classic Big Band Fest. Let's hear it for the arts!*

*From my heart to yours, remember to always support our kids. They are our future, and the future is bright. Till next time, you can share your thoughts, opinions, and epiphanies at WoozyMom@smt.com*

I stare at the picture of Shoshana Finkle-Woo for a long time. It feels like I know her, and I wish I did. She sounds like such a great mom. She drives her daughter and her friends to school every day and knows all about what's going on in her life without being pushy. She sounds so proud.

I read the story over one more time, slowly.

Without warning, a big splat lands on the picture smiling up at me. I use the sleeve of my jacket to wipe my eyes, and I can't even tell if I'm crying happy tears, or sad ones. I feel all mixed up inside. I really wish I could take out my kitten and feel his soft purring against me. I wish I could find Indira. I wish I could meet the carpool mom and ask her advice about life.

Instead, I fold up the newspaper and tuck it back in the side of the cooler, take a deep breath, stand up, turn around and head back the way I came.

My adventure wasn't what I planned, but my journal is full of sketches of the people I saw, and I wrote a really good poem on the train ride home. Also, I got to spend a day off of school having an adventure on my own, and learning some cool life lessons. I'm glad I went, but no life lesson could have prepared me for the scene I came home to.

# TWENTY-NINE

# Stachybotrys Chartarum

When the car service drops me off at the end of my street right on time, I jump out and head home just like it was an ordinary school day. I'm thinking about what I'll say when she asks me how the class picnic was. If she even remembers.

I sense it before I see it. Something's changed.

At first, I don't even see my mother's car in the driveway because of all the trucks. There's one parked in the driveway behind her car, and two on the street in front of our house. A ladder is leaning against the side of the house, workmen in white coveralls standing in clumps on the lawn, and the noisy whir of a machine that makes my teeth ache.

I press the cooler tight against me and dart around the other side of the house. The trick is to sneak in the back door and get Bari settled back into my closet before anyone notices me. Then I've got to track down my mother and find out what all the commotion is about.

I look all around to make sure there's no one there, then quickly push the back door open. My mother is standing in the doorway to the mud room, with her back to me, talking on her cell phone. I walk on my tiptoes, holding the cooler tight and whispering, "Please don't wake up yet." Bari is as quiet as a mouse.

"Achoo!" My mother reaches into her sleeve and pulls out a used tissue. "There I go again," she says into the phone. As she does, she turns around and sees me standing there. She gives me a little wave and then holds up one finger to tell me to wait. "We're tearing the house apart and not one symptom all afternoon. Now just like that, my head, achoo! sorry, feels like it's stuffed with cotton. I told Leo we're going to sue that lousy builder."

She keeps talking so I signal back that I have to go to the bathroom, and make a mad dash for my bedroom. I unzip the cooler to let Bari out, but instead of leaping out like an excited frog the way he did in the city, he stays huddled in a tight little ball in the bottom of the cooler. I reach in and try to lift him out, but he hisses at me and gives me a mad look. I decide to wait and let him climb out when he feels safe and ready. I leave the bag open there on my closet floor, turn on the light, close the door, and head downstairs to see what all the fuss is about.

It's nine o'clock by the time the workmen all leave for the day. My mother has me get a wet washcloth for her head, while she lies down on the sofa in the den. She hands me her phone and I find the meditation app that helps her fall asleep at night. I scroll through the different sounds until I find the one that is a babbling brook and set the phone down on the pillow next to her head.

We're both starving so I go into the kitchen and heat up some soup for both of us.

"I made you that creamy mushroom soup that you like and added spicy croutons," I tell her, balancing two bowls on a tray. "Do you want some tea too? Or a glass of wine?"

"Just some water," she tells me. "And could you bring me another pill? My new prescription is right next to the sink."

I cover her with a blanket and get her all settled, then sit down on the floor next to the couch, holding my soup bowl on my lap.

"I can't believe they didn't find a thing," she says. "They're coming back tomorrow with more sophisticated equipment. There is mold growing somewhere in this house and I won't rest until they find it. I cannot live like this."

I take a spoonful of my alphabet soup.

"What if they don't find it? What then?"

"Then we hire somebody else who knows what they're doing. This house must be crawling with mold spores inside the walls. How else can you explain my allergic rhinitis?"

"What?"

"Dr. King-Fisher said that's what it must be. A week ago I'm fine, then we have all this wet weather, and I develop allergies to my own house. Not to my car, not to the office, not to anything but my own moldy house."

She throws her head back against the pillow and lets out a steady stream of sneezes that shake the whole couch. When she recovers, she launches back in to her complaining. "I knew that builder was taking short cuts when he was building this rat-trap. He'll be sorry he ever worked for us, I can tell you that!" With that, she blows her nose loudly and repositions the washcloth on her forehead, then closes her eyes. Her soup is still untouched.

"Mom?"

She grunts a reply.

"How come I'm not sick? I mean if that mold is making you so sick, how come I'm not sneezing? How come I'm not sick too?"

That question makes her smile, the first smile I've seen from her all day. "Ah, my little legal eagle. You think just like a lawyer. I've taught you well." She dabs her eyes with a tissue, then continues. "There's a disgusting black mold called stachybotrys chartarum and it makes some people sick. But not everybody. At least it's not making you sneeze. Who knows what it could be doing to your lungs, though."

"My lungs!?"

"Oh, don't get so excited, Elinor. I'll be the designated worrier. And I'll take care of it one way or another. I told your father that builder was an idiot. We've got water seeping in somewhere and it's growing mold like cancer. Can you pass me my soup?"

She sits up and eats her soup like it it's a gourmet meal, then she hands the empty bowl to me and lies back down, my signal that dinner is over. I spread the blanket back over her, and turn the lights down with the dimmer switch. I put her bowl on the tray next to mine and head to the kitchen.

I rinse hers to put it in the dishwasher, but when I go to rinse mine, I see that there's still a spoonful left. I know it's not polite to drink your soup out of the bowl, but nobody's watching so I lift the bowl to my mouth. I swallow the tomatoey liquid and when I set the bowl in the sink to rinse it, I see three stubborn alphabet noodles still sticking to the side. I turn on the water and rinse a-c-t down the drain.

# Penpals, Friends, and Deathly Quiet

After I'm all settled in bed for the night, I keep going over my day in my head – sneaking out of the house with a kitten in a cooler, hanging out alone in the city, taking care of my sick mother till she fell asleep. I try to close my eyes, but there's too much swirling around inside my head.

Finally, I get up and find the newspaper that's folded up in the pocket of the cooler that's still on my closet floor. Bari has forgiven me, so I scoop him up, and climb back into bed with the paper, my laptop, and my purring sidekick. I read over the carpool column one more time, adjust the kitten on the pillow beside me, and begin.

*Dear Carpool Mom,*

*I read about you in the paper today. We don't get your paper at my house, so I never knew about you before. I just wanted to say you sound very nice. If you were my mom, I wouldn't sleep on the way to school.*
*Your faithful reader,*
*E.M.*

*ps. What's a Daisy Mae Drag? Just wondering because I'm thinking about changing my name to Daisy.*

I hit send, close the computer, and snuggle there with Bari until I fall into a deep sleep.

When I come down for school the next morning, my mother is curled on the edge of the couch drinking tea, and scrolling through her phone. Her nose is all red.

"You'll have to take the bus today. I just cannot move. I was up all night," she says when she sees me. "Bring me my purse. I'll get you some lunch money."

"Do you want your briefcase too?"

"I already called in and told Gaby to hold all my calls. I am not leaving here until they find that awful mold and get rid of it."

Her purse is on the table by the front door. I hand it to her and she hands me a twenty. "Thanks, Mom. I hope you feel better soon."

"You'd better hope I'm better, Elinor. We're not going to live in a house that's poisoning us," she says as I zip up my backpack.

"What do you mean? What if they can't get rid of the mold?"

"Oh, they'll get rid of it all right. And if they can't, we'll be suing that crooked builder for all he's worth and you'll have a new neighborhood to come home to."

"Wait, what? We have to move?" I shout over a volley of sneezes from my red-nosed mother.

"Oh, for goodness sake, Elinor. Don't be so dramatic. And hurry up or you'll miss your bus."

On the bus ride, I worry about what's happening at home. But when I get to my classroom, Christine smiles at me when I sit down next to her, and my troubles seem to just disappear.

"I like your sweater," I say.

"It's new," she says. "Thanks. Cool jeans."

I'm wearing brand new jeans with flowers embroidered on the pocket. Not counting these, I have thirteen pairs of jeans in my closet. My mother is seriously addicted to shopping.

There's a warm-up exercise on the board that we're supposed to work on till the bell rings, but instead I take out my journal and start to sketch a flower. I keep my head down, but I can feel her eyes on me, watching me draw.

"Want to come over?... Someday?... Maybe?" Christine whispers.

It feels like I am lighting up from the inside out. I wonder how red my face is. I clear my throat and then respond in my most Indira-like voice. "Okey-dokey, artichokey."

She doesn't say anything, and I'm sure she's about to laugh and tell me she was only kidding. I wonder if somebody made her invite me over as a joke. When I look up at her, she is smiling at me. "I'll ask my mom if you can come over tomorrow," she whispers just before Ms. Chasten taps her hand on my desk and says, "Page 217, Elinor. Top of the page, first column."

I open my math book and look at the first problem. I know the answer without even having to write the problem down. When the teacher moves to the other side of the room, I slip my journal on top of the open math book, and turn to the next blank page.

*Friends,* I write across the top of the page. Underneath, in my best calligraphy, I write *Indira Makepeace.*

I turn to the girl sitting next to me and focus on her. She is busily working out a math problem, but she must be able to feel my eyes on her. She lifts her head from her work, gives me a quick smile, and returns to solving the equation.

I take a deep breath. Under Indira's name I write, *Christine Corrales,* before slipping my journal back into my backpack.

All day it feels like I am floating on air.

On the way home from school, reality starts to set back in, and I prepare to be greeted by noisy workmen and lots of commotion. But when I get off the bus, it's quiet, and when I open the door, no one is there. There's no note on the table for me. It is deathly quiet.

I grab a box of crackers and head upstairs to wait. In my room, I toss my backpack on my bed and grab my laptop. When I open Google, there's an unopened email waiting for me, and my heart does a little leap.

*Dear E.M.*

*Thank you for your kind words. I like knowing that I'm touching people's lives with the letters I string together. Let your love light shine! Peacefully yours,*

*S. Finkle-Woo, Carpool Mom, Santa Marita Spirit*

I hit reply and start to type.

*Dear Carpool Mom,*

*You are the first real writer I've ever talked to and you are so lucky to write for a newspaper. I think I might be a writer too. I love poetry and I write a lot of poems. Do you know why they don't put poems in the newspaper?*

*I have two more questions for you if you're not too busy to answer. Is there really a writing gene like you said? What's a love light? Oh, and also, did you forget to answer about the Daisy Mae Drag thing? Because I still don't know what it is.*

*Your faithful reader,*
*E.M.*

After I hit send, I close the laptop and walk towards my closet. I can't wait to tell Bari everything that's happened today. A wave of weirdness comes over me as I grab the handle of the closet door.

Something is just not right. It feels like all the air has been sucked out of my room. I open the closet door and switch on the light. It is way too quiet in there. Deathly quiet.

Where's Bari?

# THIRTY-ONE

# Easy/Messy/Exciting

My mother always says, when it rains it pours, and at the moment, I am definitely feeling like my life is a monsoon and thunderstorm all rolled up into one big flash flood.

Problem number one: My mother got an allergy shot yesterday and is under doctor's orders to give her system a chance to recover before coming home, so she's holed up in a fancy hotel in the city, ordering room service and resting.

When the doctor told her to stay out of the house for a few days, she said she was going to stay at the Victorian Inn downtown and I could stay with her. I love hotels.

Last night I heard her on the phone with my dad, yelling about the mold. "He said there was no mold anywhere. Told me, this house is sealed tight as a drum – not a bit of moisture anywhere. He must be in cahoots with that builder. He does not know who he's dealing with though!" Then she started sneezing so much that she had to hang up.

Problem number two: The next thing I knew, my dad cancelled his business trip, and told my mother she should take advantage of the situation and take a little luxury spa-cation at the Hilton in the city. "It's just you and me, kid!" he told me when he got home. "We can stay up late and order pizza!"

Normally, I'd be all excited, but having a missing pet does things to a person's mood. I wanted to tell him about Bari, because my dad is the world's best finder of lost objects, but my heart was really hurting and I stormed out of the room when he said it was just him and me and pizza. I ran upstairs and slammed the door.

My dad knocked a few minutes later, and poked his head in. "What's the matter, love? How can I help?"

I should have told him then, but instead I just started yelling, "It's not fair! It's not fair!" I might have been a little hysterical.

He gave me a surprised look and shook his head. "Sometimes I just don't understand women!" he said. "I'll let you cool off. Come down when you're ready." And with that, he closed my door.

Problem number three: My mother always tells me that calamities come in threes and she is right as rain, because this is the biggest calamity of my entire life. Bari is still missing. His bowl and his food and his toys are all untouched in my closet.

I cry myself to sleep and dream that when I wake up in the morning, he's snuggled in his little cat bed in the closet.

I wake up to the sound of my dad talking on the speaker phone and the sun edging into the room. I get up and check the closet first. Bari is sound asleep in there. He just has to be. But. He. Is. Not.

I keep telling myself that he just got a little spooked with all those workmen banging on the house, and now that it's nice and quiet again he'll show up.

But then the what if's start ringing in my ears. What if he's really lost? What if he's too scared to find his way back? What if he's really hurt?

In third grade we had to do author's chair and read a story to the whole class that we wrote in writers' workshop. This girl named Brianna wrote about how her new kitten somehow climbed into the wall behind the kitchen cabinets and they heard a mewing that at first she thought was a ghost. They had to remove the cabinet to rescue the kitten and it cost a lot of money. The title of her story was "My Million Dollar Baby."

What if Bari is trapped inside the wall from when the workmen were here?

I have never cut school before, but then I have never had a missing pet before. I can't sit through a whole day of school knowing he might be scared or lost or hurt in our big old house. I yell bye to my dad as I'm closing the front door. I walk like normal to the corner, then dash across Mrs. Feinstein's back yard, and tiptoe as stealthily as a cat to the side door of our house. I find the fake rock in the garden where we hide a key for emergencies, but the key isn't there. How can I sneak back inside if all the doors are locked and my dad's still in there?

I sit down in a flower bed and lean against house. My heart is pounding and I can't figure out what to do so I take out my journal and make a list of options.

Ring the doorbell and tell Dad I missed the bus and ask him to drive me to school. (easiest)

Sit in the garden all day till school gets out and hope the sprinklers don't come on. (messiest)

Take the train to the city and try to find Indira at her school. (excitingest)

I know before I even finish writing down that third option, that it's the only one that makes sense. This is a job for the Sleuthadelic Detective Agency! Indira will know what to do. I put away my journal, take out my cell phone, and click on the MovingKids app.

Twenty minutes later, I'm on the train to the city. There's no looking back. I feel like a criminal and keep waiting for somebody to ask me why I'm not in school, but nobody does.

I know about the morning crowds now, and I've made sure to stand right next to the door for the entire ride. Even when people push and pull, climbing on and off the train, I plant my feet and stay glued to my spot so that when it finally stops and the loudspeaker shouts, "Theater District," I'm ready. I do not want to wander around aimlessly again.

I step off the train into the bustle of the city. It is always noisy and in motion here, and a feeling like love floods my heart. I walk to the Ballet Academy entrance and run my hand across the sign that says *Santa Marita Ballet Academy: Ring for Entry.* Why is my heart pounding so ferociously?

It feels like there is electricity inside me and I'm wired to this building. I take a step back on the sidewalk and stare at the giant poster, encased in glass, hanging next to the door. There are three girls in tutus and toe shoes, smiling at the camera, smiling right at me. My heart is beating out of my chest and my throat is dry.

I will not cry. Instead, I turn away and head to the park. I know Indira won't be there yet, but I sit on the bench by the fountain where I first saw her all those months ago. I take out the little bluebird and hold it tight in my hand for a few minutes, concentrating, then slide it back into my pocket. I close my eyes and picture Bari purring in my lap, until I know that he's safe at home.

My journal feels like an old friend in my hands when I take it out of my backpack and start to sketch. I sit there, sketching and writing for a long time. The sun is warm against my neck, and the park is filled with happy sounds. If I were a cat, I'd be purring. This is my favorite place on the planet. I wonder what I'm missing at school.

# Searching

How hard can it be to find someone who's not lost? I know if I just concentrate, I can find Indira's school. And if I can find her school, I'm sure I can find her. I just hope her school is not near the Hilton. I would not want to be me if my mom were stepping out for fresh air and ran into me on the sidewalk when I'm an hour away from home in the middle of the morning on a school day. That would not be pretty. I will have to pay really close attention to my surroundings.

First, I walk to the middle of the park and stand as still as a statue. I drop my backpack to the ground and take a deep breath, close my eyes, and push my hands together in front of me until I feel perfectly at peace. I wait there in stillness until it feels like my third eye space is opening up, and there's Indira, smiling at me inside my head.

I open my eyes, pick up my backpack and head out of the park. I cross the street and just start walking, following my nose. Pretty soon I'm walking down a street that looks like a giant sidewalk sale. Every store has a table on the sidewalk in front with boxes of stuff to buy. There are plastic frogs and backscratchers, coffee cups and tee shirts with weird sayings, jewelry boxes and spinning racks of postcards. I want to walk by quickly because I'm on a mission to find Indira, but the stuff on the street slows me down. I want to stop and look at everything.

I pause in front of a display of windchimes playing the softest tinkling music, even though there is no wind. It sounds like pure happiness, so I ask the man standing in the doorway to take one down for me.

"Namaste," he says, bowing as he hands it to me.

"Merci," I say back, then go inside the store to buy it from a small wrinkled woman behind the counter who doesn't smile at me or say a word. I slip my purchase into my backpack and head back outside. Every step I take is accompanied by the jingle of a wordless soundtrack that makes me feel like I'm floating through the crowd on my quest to find Indira.

As I walk, the scene begins to change. The shops are set further back from the street, and the sidewalks are wide and flat, shaded by white-blossomed trees. Even the store windows look different here, sparkling clean to show off elaborate displays. There's an entire miniature farmyard populated with stuffed animals, a fancy table decorated with a three-tiered cake and china plates holding fancy desserts, and a storefront window filled with real sand and little rainbow-colored umbrellas. I know I've landed in the ritzy part of town, and I'm just about to turn around when I spot her.

She is walking along with a whole group of teenagers crossing the street in front of me on the next corner. It's the weirdest thing though. There are all these kids walking together in a clump, and then there's Indira. She's with them, but not, all at the same time. When they get to my side of the street, the clump walks into a café on the corner called Il Fortuna, but Indira keeps walking. She enters another doorway two doors down, and I follow right on her heels.

This is too good to be true. It's my good karma, I think, and I decide to surprise her. I'll just follow her inside and stroll up to her casually like it's no big deal. Maybe she'll even let me walk back to school with her and meet Ms. Fris and all her friends. Or maybe she'll want to skip school this afternoon and head back to my house with me to find Bari. The windchimes in my backpack play a lively little jig as I move.

I can see Indira through the window of this place called Nekktar Bar. I can't believe my luck, standing in the doorway of this crowded space, filled with the noise of laughter and whirring blenders. Indira is standing in line behind a tall boy who is kind of dancing in time to his own beat. I am scanning the room for an empty table so we can sit and talk. And then it happens.

The tall boy moves up to the counter to order his wheatgrass shake, and Indira inches forward, changing my view of the room.

There is a woman hunched over a laptop at the corner table, madly tapping away. Her back is to me, but she looks out of place in this casual spot where everyone is sipping on their liquid lunch and listening to hip-hop. She's wearing a suit and her hair looks like a spiky helmet. I'd know the back of that head anywhere.

A shiver passes through my whole body and I bolt back out the door with my backpack clanging madly behind me. I run down the street and duck into the nearest doorway.

"Welcome to the Hilton, Miss," says a man in a blood red uniform.

# Help!

Dear Carpool Mom,

I'm sorry to bother you again, but I need to talk to someone and I feel like you are a good listener. I don't even know where to start, but here goes. I keep doing all these really dumb things and no one even knows I'm bad. Today I went to the city to meet somebody but I didn't get a chance because I almost got caught being a criminal. I sort of skipped school which I had to do because I actually really just wanted to find my lost cat. And that's another story because nobody even knows I have a cat. I wonder what you would do if you ever found out your daughter was doing all these disappointing things behind your back.

*I don't know why I keep doing bad stuff. It feels like I'm a ping-pong ball or something, do you know what I mean?*

*Anyway, you don't have to answer this. I just wanted to tell somebody. Actually, I told my cat and he licked my face, but you know, he's not a real person.*

*Your faithful reader,*

*E.M.*

## THIRTY-FOUR
# A New Leaf

**B**ari slept on my chest all night, and I could feel his little heart beating in time with mine. I wish I knew where he was all that time when he was missing. That's the thing about cats I guess; you can tell them all your secrets, but they can't tell you anything back. It's like he has his own secret life that I'll never know about. All I know is that when I got home from the city yesterday afternoon, he was curled up asleep in his little cat bed in my closet, just like I had pictured him.

I had a hard time falling asleep with all these mixed up feelings inside me. I had some scary dreams too of running, and being lost, and not being able to find my way home. But the sun is shining this morning, and today will be a different. I am done doing bad things. Today I'm just going to count my blessings.

First of all, I know I am lucky and have good karma. So that's a blessing. I am the best kind of spy because I didn't get caught. Blessing with a capital b. I got to see Indira living her real life and she didn't even sense that I was there. So that was sort of cool. And I was this close to my mother, but she didn't turn around or know that I was right behind her when I was supposed to be in school. That was even cooler. And, I pictured my cat being safe at home and he was. Triple cool. Blessings cubed.

But the best part of this new day is the message I found in my email when I woke up. A real live writer knows who I am and takes the time to answer my questions. That is x-factor cool, blessings to the nth degree.

> *E.M. Dear,*
>
> *Everybody makes mistakes. Everybody. But you should not keep secrets. It bottles up the spirit and causes pain. So, here's my advice. Turn over a new leaf starting today. Take charge of your happiness. Be your best self. Don't tell lies or sneak around. And for goodness sake, don't take your education for granted again. You must learn to write your own story.*
>
> *p.s. Girls ask boys to the Daisy Mae Drag. It's an outdated tradition, but I think of it as a sort of feminist empowerment. I asked Chester*

*Woo to the Daisy Mae Drag twenty-one years ago and we've lived happily ever after ever since. You never know what happiness might be waiting just around the bend.*
*Your friend in peace, love, and harmony,*
*S. Finkle-Woo, Carpool Mom, Santa Marita Spirit*

Today I will be my best self. I will start writing my own story because today is the first day of the rest of my life. I repeat it over and over, chanting it like a mantra. I believe it deep inside my bones.

I sit down at my desk and draw a green leaf full of veins and brimming with life-giving chlorophyll. A leaf bursting with life and the promise of springtime. *Today is the first day of the rest of my life* I write on one side. I flip the leaf over and write my name on the other side: *Elinor (Daisy) Malcolm,* then tape it into my journal under today's date. I am turning over a new leaf, starting now.

I open my laptop and read the message from Carpool Mom one more time. Okay, I think, I am not ready for a boyfriend, but I could definitely use a close friend to hang out with at school. I decide to write Christine a haiku.

*You asked me over*
*Yesterday I wasn't here*
*What about today?*

I decorate the page with squiggles and smiley faces, then put it in my homework folder, put my folder in my backpack, and finish getting ready for school.

## THIRTY-FIVE
# Word Nerds

After lunch today, instead of hanging out in the library, I am walking all around the blacktop with Christine. We are playing this game she invented called Name that Kid. The trick is to use as few words as possible to describe somebody. Like for Stuart Henry, all you have to say is "teeth" and the other person will know who you mean. Or for Andrea Romero, if you say "boobs" everyone will know it's her. It's sort of mean, I guess, but I think it's kind of like poetry too, if you think about it.

"We're the best kind of nerds," she tells me. "We're word nerds."

I wonder if there's just one word to describe me. And what would it be? I want to ask Christine that, but I don't. Instead I make up a rhyming game, which we're both really good at.

"This is the best time I've ever had at recess," I tell her when the bell rings.

"Yup, we're just a couple of poemcrazy chicks," she says.

I wish I could tell her about how I'm turning over a new leaf, but I don't want to jinx it. It seems like if you talk about it, it won't count anymore. Kind of like if you tell your wish after you blow out your birthday candles. I wish she could meet Indira or read the messages from Carpool Mom, but I guess everybody has a special part they keep secret.

Yesterday after school I got to go to Christine's house, which is the coolest house in the whole world if you ask me. Everywhere you look is a reminder that somebody lives there. There are piles of folded laundry on all the beds, stacks of books piled high on bookshelves and on every tabletop, and chocolate chip cookies fresh out of the oven, cooling on the counter.

Christine has two brothers and two dogs, a turtle named Mildred who lives in an aquarium in the boys' room, and a noisy miniature parrot named Elbird that lives in a cage in her room. The house is just happy and full of life if you know what I mean.

Outside is just like an extension of the inside with lots of reminders of who lives there. There are bikes and basketballs and skateboards all along the side of the house, and fruit trees and overflowing wooden flower pots all across the backyard. I wish Indira could see this place. She'd probably say, "This house is alive. It has a heartbeat that you can hear if you listen." I know she'd feel right at home here.

"Let's hang out at your house tomorrow," Christine says as I'm climbing in the back seat of her mother's car to go home.

Miraculously, even though it's my mother's first day back home since her time at the Hilton, she tells me that it's okay if Christine comes over. She even says we can order pizza and watch a movie in the den.

"I can't wait to meet your little friend," she says, and I think she really means it.

Christine is the first friend I've had over since third grade when Candice Kane spilled black ink on the family room carpet. That was like a scene out of a horror movie, with my mother totally losing it and Candice locking herself in the bathroom until her nanny came and took her home.

And Indira doesn't count because she just showed up out of the blue and my parents never even knew she was here. I wish she lived closer so we could hang out, but she has her life in the city and I have my life here in Maple Meadows. She's still my best friend in the whole world though.

But now Christine is here, eating dinner in the dining room. I think she's my second best friend. My mother bought us soda to have with our pizza and she's trying really hard to be nice and friendly. She hasn't sneezed once since we got home.

Dad is doing his interview routine, making Christine laugh. He says it's important to ask people lots of questions when you first meet them to show you're interested.

"Is it Christine Corrales or Christine Corral-more?"

"Did you say you have two turtles and one brother who lives in an aquarium?"

"What kind of a person can teach a bird to talk but doesn't know how to speak bird?"

See what I mean? We laugh all through dinner and it feels like I have the perfect family. The perfect life. Turning over a new leaf is really working.

After dinner, when I show Christine my room and let her play with my little kitten, I bet it'll seal the deal. We'll be friends for life.

Maybe I'll even tell her some of my secret stuff. I wonder if we'll be able to figure out a way for her to meet Indira. I bet if she did, we'd be like the three amigos, three word-loving, poemcrazy chicks.

# THIRTY-SIX

# Shenanigans

y house is just my house, so it seems perfectly normal to me. But Christine has said "Wow!" a hundred times since she got here. "Wow!" when she walked through the front door, "Wow!" when we walked into the kitchen, "Wow!" when I showed her where the bathroom is, and "Wow!" when I opened the fridge.

But, when I open the door to my room after dinner, she is completely silent. Christine just stands there with her mouth wide open, staring. Finally, she turns to me and says, "You are so lucky, Elinor. This is amazing!"

It's just my room.

"I have something to show you that really is amazing," I say. "You won't believe your eyes!" She follows me into my room and plunks onto my bed. "Can you keep a secret?" I walk to the closet and turn the knob slowly.

"Oh, my gosh!" she says. "This closet is as big as my whole room! Wow!"

"That's not what I wanted to show you. Come here. Take a look."

I point to the back of my closet which I've transformed into a little kitty hotel. And there, curled up on a blanket is Bari, my little soft orange ball of fluff.

"A kitten!" she shouts.

"Ssshh!" I whisper. "It's a secret. I'm not allowed to have any pets because my mother thinks they're full of diseases. Nobody else knows I have him. Just you. Oh, and one other person, but she's a secret too."

"Awww, can I hold him?" Christine asks, and before I can answer she lunges toward him. Bari wakes with a start, gives a frightened kitty yelp, and speeds right past us into my bedroom.

I see the open door a second after he does, the door that I forgot to close, the door that leads right out into the open hallway. The door that Bari speeds through with Christine in hot pursuit.

"Stop!" I shout. "Don't chase him. You'll make it worse!"

The door to my parents' bedroom flies open, and there stands my mother in her fuzzy white robe and shower cap, her face covered with white goop. "Elinor! What on earth? What is all this racket?"

Christine and I freeze there in our tracks. "Sorry," I say. "We were just playing a game. We'll calm down."

"Well, for pity sake. I have had a trying week and I just need a good long soak. I do not need all these shenanigans in my own home. You can tell your father that it's time to take your little friend home." She turns and heads into the bathroom where the tub is nearly overflowing. "Now. Wouldn't that have just been a perfect end to all our house troubles?" she yells as she reaches for the tap.

"But, Mom!"

She turns off the water and steps out of her slippers.

"Goodnight, Elinor."

Behind me, Christine is on the floor, looking under the bed and stage-whispering, "Here, kitty kitty. Nice kitty."

I quickly run through the possibilities in my head. I think about the new leaf I've turned over, and the new friend who I don't want to lose. I swallow hard, and take a deep breath. "Sorry, Mom. We'll leave you in peace now. Night."

I reach out to close the door between the bathroom and the bedroom, just as Christine screams and a furry force of nature whizzes past me right into the path of my hysterical, screaming mother.

# THIRTY-SEVEN

# Morality Play

I never knew Christine was such a fast thinker. After my mother stopped shouting about her fear of cats and her terrible allergies and lice and fleas and all of that, Christine did the most noble thing ever.

"Sorry, Mrs. Malcolm," she said. "It's all my fault. Elinor told me you had a no pet rule, but I just wanted her to see my new kitten so I snuck him in here in my backpack. I'm really sorry. I'll be going now. I didn't mean to upset you."

And even with all that, my mother still said in her most embarrassing tone, "You think that's all it takes, just a half-hearted apology and everything's hunky-dory? Just an I'm sorry, Mrs. Malcolm and all's forgiven? Let me tell you a little something about how the world works." The white goop on her face had hardened and made her look really scary. But even with all that, Christine stayed loyal and true, keeping her head down and looking remorseful.

I've never had a friend like that.

"We're all very lucky that I had an allergy shot this morning or the paramedics would be on their way. I am severely allergic to cats. Do you understand? Severely!"

"I'm so sorry, Mrs. Malcolm. I didn't know. I'm so sorry," she continued as she scooped up Bari and backed toward the doorway. "Could Mr. Malcolm just take me home now?"

So now here I am, sitting on my bed, all cried out, without even a kitten to hold. I'm faced with a decision that might be the biggest decision of my life. I open my journal and touch the leaf that I taped there just a week ago. I keep saying I'm turning over a new leaf, but so far it's just the same old lying, cheating me. I could never be brave like Christine. But I want to try.

I take a deep breath, swallow hard, get myself centered and decide it's time to go knock on my mother's door and come clean. I'm going to tell her everything.

But, just as I climb off my bed and start to cross my bedroom floor, I hear a little tune coming from my backpack in the corner. My cell phone is ringing and it's Christine.

"We need to talk," she tells me. "I have a plan."

# THIRTY-EIGHT

# Seventeen Syllables

D ear Carpool Mom,

I tried to do what you said. I turned over a new leaf, but it's not working. What would you do if somebody you knew was allergic to your cat, but you knew if they got an allergy shot they wouldn't die? Would you keep the cat and tell them to please keeping getting the shots, or would you give the cat to somebody who would love it just as much as you and would let you visit anytime? If you don't know, maybe you could ask your daughter Tiffany what she would do if she had a cat and you were allergic.

My mother turns red
She can't breathe because of me
But she gave me life

That's a haiku I wrote tonight. Sometimes poetry helps, but not tonight. Writing to you helps though. Thank you for listening.

Your faithful reader,

E.M.

# THIRTY-NINE

# Healing Hearts

This is the coolest thing that's ever happened to me. Christine and I are at this all-day festival in the city. Her mom is here too but she agreed to let us walk around by ourselves. We just had to promise to meet her back in the Centering Room every forty-five minutes.

We're in a big old warehouse that's been transformed into The Healing HeARTs: A Mystical Festival for the Senses. The Carpool Mom has a booth here which is how I found out about it. Her paper, *The Santa Marita Spirit*, is one of the sponsors, and Shoshana Finkle-Woo herself invited me to come check it out.

When she answered my last email she told me about an organization she started called "The Healing HeARTs." She says you're supposed to use art to become a better person, somebody she calls an enlightened planet-dweller. And she said there's plenty of food for those who hunger for truth. I'm trying to always tell the truth, but it's hard.

The Carpool Mom said she knew I'd like it because of my poetic voice and heart. At first I thought about asking my mother to take me, but she's not crazy about touchy-feely stuff. She thinks it's kind of weird actually. But then when I told Christine, she got all excited and said her mom has an artsy spirit and maybe she could take us. Her mom said it sounded like a cool way to spend a Saturday, so here we are.

We walk by all these booths selling crystals and oils and books. There's an exhibit hall that has different classes throughout the day. We walk by the Art of Music for Massage, Spiritual Endurance, and Yoga for Life. A little further down the hall is Tai Chi for Beginners and Writing: Exercise for a Healthy Heart. Everything sounds so interesting; we can't decide where to go first. Then Christine spots a sign for a dancing poetry performance that starts in fifteen minutes.

"Hey, check this out," she says, pointing to the sign. "Dancing poetry! Sounds like it's tailor-made for two poemcrazy chicks!"

It's amazing how much alike Christine and I are. She used to take ballet too. "Look at this, Elinor," she says.

"It says that the dancers take original poetry and present it through music. We'll have to pay close attention. I bet we could learn to do something like this for the talent show."

It feels so good to have a friend who thinks like I do and loves to do all the same things. I tell Christine if it wasn't for her I'd be sitting all alone in my room feeling sorry for myself. She saved me from a life of crime by adopting Bari for a while. She calls herself his foster mom. He sleeps in her room, right on her bed, and he gets to roam around outside with her brothers and the dogs. She says he is not interested in the bird or the turtle which is kind of unusual for a feline. He's always been a very special cat.

When she first came up with her plan, I thought I would be so sad without Bari, but it's a strange thing. As long as I know he's safe, it's okay that he has someplace else to live. And now that I have Christine to talk to every day, I don't need a cat so much. It would be sort of fun to have a bird though. Maybe one day.

I wish I could be brave like Christine though. I really wanted to tell my mother about having a kitten, and how everything that happened was my fault, but I'm so scared of disappointing her and my dad. Turning over as new leaf is harder than it sounds.

Christine is tugging on my arm. "Come on," she says, "let's go find where this dance thing is, and get good seats. I don't want to miss it."

We turn down another aisle, following the crowd. I'm trying to picture what my mother would think of this place if she was here. She hasn't been one bit tired or sneezy since Bari moved to Christine's house. She just keeps saying stuff like, "You know, that stay at the Hilton really calmed my immune system. That insurance company should thank their lucky stars. After all, a week at the Hilton is a lot cheaper than the alternatives!" I wonder what she'd do if she knew I was the one who was responsible for her getting sick and for her getting better.

We pass by a booth for the Santa Marita Spirit, but it's empty. I have to find the Carpool Mom today so I can thank her in person for changing my life. I want to introduce her to Christine on this perfect day. The only thing that would make it even more perfect would be if Indira was here. This day would be right up her alley.

Christine points to a little room at the very back of the warehouse where the lights are flashing on and off. "Let's go!" she says. "This is it. It must be starting!"

There are about twenty folding chairs set up facing a little wooden stage. We take our seats in the back row. "We can sneak out without disturbing anybody if it's too weird or if it's time to meet my mom," Christine says.

Two small speakers are hanging from the ceiling and a microphone is dangling above the stage. The rooms grows pitch dark and a woman's voice from the speakers says,

"Welcome friends, to the first ever dance of life presented by the Healing HeARTs. What you're witnessing today is a unique art form, introduced for your enlightenment and pure enjoyment by the wonderfully creative, one and only, Tiffany Zara Woo. Tiffany has taken four original poems and choreographed them into a living, breathing dance of life. Here now, with no further ado, we present this moment of inspiration for your heart and mind, the dance."

The lights go on, and there is a small lump in the center of the stage. For nearly five minutes that seem like an eternity, there is no motion, but no one in the audience moves either.

"I don't get it," Christine whispers. "Is this part of the dance?"

"I'm not sure, but it's way too weird for me."

"Let's go. It's almost time to meet my mom anyway."

Christine and I both start to rise when the music starts and the lights flicker. A screech of violins. The lump on the stage stretches out, arms reaching high above her head, legs stretched out long, toes pointed. The lump is a long, stiff body pinned to the floor, covered with a sheet. Then the arms swoop up, off the ground. The music stops. "Huh-huh-huh-huh," the stretched out lump on the stage breathes out these four loud, exaggerated breaths.

Christine and I sit back down, transfixed.

"This I gotta see," Christine whispers to me.

My skin is electrified.

The dancer does a slow-motion somersault backwards, then stands up like she's in a trance. She's wearing a red unitard and her face is a red mask. The violins start again, this time slow and mournful, and the dancer moves slowly, dreamlike.

The voice from the speakers begins to sing.

*"My mother, my mother, my mother, my mother*
*Turns red, yes red, I say red, so red, fire red, blood red*
*My mother turns red*
*She can't…"*

The dancer falls to the ground and breathes those four exaggerated breaths again.

"Elinor, this is too weird," Christine says as she starts to stand up again.

"Ssshh," I say and push her back into her seat.

The hair on my neck is standing straight up.

"Because of me!" the dancer on the stage roars, making everyone in the audience jump. Then she lies back down in the middle of the stage.

"That's my poem," I whisper to Christine. I am shaking like a leaf.

"What?"

"I wrote it. That's my poem."

"Okay," Christine says but I can tell by the way she says it that she thinks I'm making it up.

We watch the rest of the poetry dance, but I am not paying much attention. I'm lost in my thoughts, trying to figure out how my poem got to the stage in this weird dance. What force brought me here to witness it.

Every time I think I've got life figured out, I'm reminded that there are forces greater than me in the world. Some things are just too complicated and mysterious to understand. I'm thinking about all of this until I hear the audience applauding and see that Christine is standing next to me. The voice through the speakers says, "Thank you for coming, fellow planet-dwellers. Don't forget to stop by our booth today for information on how you can be part of our movement. It's not too soon to find out how you can be part of next year's Healing HeARTs Festival. Go now, in peace and harmony."

We find Christine's mother in the Centering Room and both try to tell her about the strange dance we've just seen. "And Elinor thinks it was her poem they were dancing to," Christine tells her.

"It was. It was my poem. If we can find the lady from the newspaper, she'll tell you. I sent it to her. She'll tell you."

"The lady in the Santa Marita Spirit booth?" asks Christine's mom. "Follow me. I know just where that is."

# I AM E.M.

Right away I recognize her from her picture in the newspaper. The Carpool Mom is sitting at a table inside a booth decorated with hearts.

She looks up at me and she has the kindest eyes. "I'm Elinor. Elinor Malcolm. You know, E.M.?"

I put out my hand and she grabs it with both of hers. Her hands are warm and soft. She holds on and looks at me intently.

"I wondered what the E.M. stood for. Elinor. Elinor Malcolm. What a lovely name. Pleased to meet you, Elinor Malcolm." Her voice sounds so familiar. So do her eyes. She has a smile that lights up her whole face, and crinkly happy eyes. "And this must be your lovely mother."

"Oh, no," Christine's mom says. "Although she's almost like a daughter to me. I'm Jo. Jo Corrales. And this is my daughter Christine."

The Carpool Mom shakes their hands too. We all start talking at once, saying what a cool experience this has been. "I don't think we've ever experienced anything like this before," Christine's mom says.

"Well, I'm sorry your mom couldn't be here, Elinor," she says. "I'd really like to meet the mother of such an extraordinary kid. Did you get to see your poem dance?"

I look at Christine, who nods her head at me and mouths the word "wow!"

"But how?…"

The Carpool Mom laughs. "My daughter. I showed it to her and she said I've just got to create a dance to this. And then she told me her idea about a dancing poetry performance here. Let me go get her. You've got to meet her. Talk about extraordinary."

"Wow!" Christine says out loud as the Carpool Mom goes through the brown curtain at the back of her booth. "You're famous, Elinor. You're the real deal!"

"Now I'm sorry I missed it, Elinor," Christine's mom says. "You girls will have to recite it for me later."

"Actually, Mom, it's more like perform instead of recite. But yeah, we'll do it for you later. It's wild. We're thinking about doing something like that for the spring talent show."

Carpool Mom is laughing as she pushes her way back through the curtain into the booth. "Here she is ladies. This is my Tiffany, mistress of the dance!"

A tall girl in a red unitard steps through the curtain. She is not wearing a mask now.

Our eyes lock.

"Elinor!"

"Indira!"

"Indira?" Christine, her mom, and the Carpool Mom all exclaim in unison.

"Yipes, stripes, where do I begin?" says Indira as she hugs her mom. "Where do I begin?"

# Normal

On the way home in the car I'm in the back seat pretending to be asleep, but my brain has never been more awake. This truly was the first day, the very best first day of the rest of my life.

Christine and her mom are talking quietly in the front seat.

"Promise you'll always tell me the truth," her mom says.

"Promise," Christine whispers. I wonder what she's thinking.

I'm going over every detail of the day in my head.

Indira does not look like somebody named Tiffany Zara Woo. But she is. I wonder why she never told her mom how hard it is to be the daughter of a newspaper columnist who has her whole life told in embarrassing detail to a bunch of strangers. Her mom cried when she found out she pretended to be someone else.

It's so much better to tell people how you feel. Not easier, just better.

We all went to a little tea room and talked about the mysteries of life. I couldn't believe when we were leaving and her mom called her Indira. "It suits you," she said. "And you have my word, I'll never write about Tiffany's exploits again."

I take my bluebird of happiness out of my pocket and hold it in my palm there in the backseat of Christine's car. I open one eye and look at it. Then I close that eye and open the other. The bird looks like it is moving back and forth, but I know it's not. It's just my perception that's changing. The bird is perfectly still.

That's one of life's little mysteries, I guess.

Indira is a mystery to me too. She knows all these things about the universe, but deep down she's just a weird girl like me who wants to be happy. Maybe everyone's the same deep down. Maybe I really am normal.

Christine's mom said she's going to drive us to the city next month so we can visit with Indira if it's all right with my mother. We're going to choreograph some more of our poems and see if we can dance them out. We'll be three poem-crazy chicks.

But first things first.

The first thing I'm going to do when I get home tonight is have a heart-to-heart talk with my mom. There's a lot she doesn't know about me. There's probably a lot I don't know about her too.

It's time to change that.

SNEAK PREVIEW
OF THE SEQUEL TO

# Elinormal

COMING IN SPRING
## 2022!

# New Girl

## the Further Adventures of Elinormal

by Kate McCarroll Moore

# ONE

# Nightmare

"**R**un, Elinor. Put some mustard on it!"
I was panting alongside my mother as we dashed through the airport from concourse B to C, my backpack slamming against me with each step along the moving walkway.

Five minutes earlier we'd been dropped at the curb by her car service, only to find our gate had been changed to a whole other part of the airport. And the plane was leaving in twenty-four minutes.

"I'm running in heels for pity's sake. At least you can keep up with me. I'm not missing this flight because of you!"

"Excuse me. Excuse me, coming through," I shouted as I followed her and her rolling suitcase careening past the people standing still on the right.

It wasn't until we were wedged into our seats in coach, my backpack crammed beneath the seat in front of me, that I could finally breathe. And only then did I start to cry.

Today was supposed to be the first day of seventh grade.

"Now what? We made it. Why are you blubbering?"

I wiped my nose with the back of my hand and swallowed hard. "I'm just so sad about Grandma Ruth."

She patted my hand and said, "Oh, I know, kiddo. Me too, me too." Then she pulled her eye shade down, popped her earbuds in, and tipped her seat back as far as it could go.

I pulled out my sketchbook and started to draw. First, I sketched me in my first day of seventh grade outfit which I was now wearing on a plane to Oklahoma for my grandma's funeral. Then I tried to draw Grandma Ruth, but it was hard to remember what she looked like. I hadn't seen her since I was nine.

Just the night before, I had gone through my closet, trying on each new outfit in front of the mirror, trying to settle on the look I was going for – cool girl, sporty girl, brainy girl – finally landing on an orange minidress, denim jacket, and white sneakers that seemed to say, "just me, Elinor Malcolm, normal girl." I hung the dress in the bathroom, draped the jacket over the back of my desk chair, and put the sneakers next to my backpack which I emptied and rearranged fifty times. I checked my vision board and whispered each hope over and over.

*Get straight A's*
*Go out for yearbook*
*Become vegan*
*Learn Spanish*
*Make new friends*

This was going to be my year. My best friend Christine and I had almost matching schedules and were going to be in three classes together. And her mom signed us both up to take a Saturday yoga class at The Healing HeARTs where my friend Indira works.

But then, just as I was getting ready to head for the bus, my mom let out a blood-curdling scream. I ran into her bedroom to find her on her knees, clutching her cell phone.

I helped her up and had her sit on the bed. Her face was pale and she was shaking.

"Mom, what is it? What happened?"

"It's Grandma Ruth," she whispered, "dead." She handed me the phone. "Call Dad and tell him we're on the next flight to Tulsa. And bring me an aspirin."

That set this nightmare in motion. Soon I was unpacking my backpack full of gel pens and labeled notebooks and a brand-new laptop, and replacing them with toiletries and underwear, and exchanging my first week of seventh grade for a funeral for a woman I barely knew.

By the time we landed and I took my phone off airplane mode, I had sixteen texts from Christine.

*Where are you?*

*Are you sick?*

*We have science homework already.*

*Where are you?*

*The cafeteria smells disgusting.*

*We have to give speeches in English.*

*And read 8 books.*

*Where are you?*

*There's a new boy from Mexico or Modesto.*

*I forgot.*

*Sort of cute.*

*Tiff Tilton got braces.*

*Janna Faz got boobs.*

*Where are you?*

*Text me.*

*Are you ok?*

My one and only first day of seventh grade was happening without me.

# ABOUT THE Author

Kate McCarroll Moore has been writing since she was a little girl. When she grew up, she became a teacher and a librarian and a poet and a mom. She never grows tired of people-watching and eavesdropping, using her writer's imagination to turn ordinary events into unique characters with interesting stories to tell.

When Kate's daughters were young, she spent countless hours dreaming up stories in the back of dance studios and recital halls while they practiced and performed. This story began, as many stories do, as an overheard conversation and a scribble across a convenient page. That's how Elinor Malcolm came to life. This is her story.

Kate grew up in upstate New York and now lives with her family in the San Francisco Bay Area.

Download an Educator Guide from
www.CityofLightPublishing.com

**Become a citizen of the City of Light!**
Follow @CityofLightPublishing